Anna Mulford

A Sketch of Dr. John Smith Sage, of Sag-Harbor, N.Y.

Anna Mulford

A Sketch of Dr. John Smith Sage, of Sag-Harbor, N.Y.

ISBN/EAN: 9783744796682

Printed in Europe, USA, Canada, Australia, Japan

Cover: Foto ©Andreas Hilbeck / pixelio.de

More available books at **www.hansebooks.com**

A SKETCH

—OF—

DR. JOHN SMITH SAGE,

OF SAG=HARBOR, N. Y.,

—BY—

ANNA MULFORD,

—WITH AN—

APPENDIX,

Containing some interesting letters of his father, Dr. Ebenezer Sage, written in the early part of the century,
and other matters relating to Sag-Harbor.

SAG-HARBOR:
J. H. HUNT, PRINTER.

1897

CONTENTS.

—:o:—

INTRODUCTION.

——:o:——

To the Reader :

While thinking of by-gone days, Dr. Sage and my aunt Eliza Gracie Dering seem to appear as clear as a dew-drop glittering in the light of an early sun-beam.

This sketch was written for my own gratification, but if you knew the Doctor something of interest may be found within these leaves.

A. M.

DR. JOHN SAGE.

——:o:——

CHAPTER 1.

ANCESTORS.

On the east bank of the Connecticut river, where it sweeps around a bend opposite the city of Middletown, Conn., the picturesque town of Portland is situated. In Colonial times it was called Chatham. About fifty years since, when the Portland stone, which is found here, was becoming popular, the name was changed to that of Portland, after a place in England, famous for freestone quarries.

Chatham was the home of John Sage's American ancestors. It is claimed by descendants that they came from France and were Huguenots, also that the name has been corrupted from La Sarge. David Sage, his grandfather, was its first Representative to the General Assembly, and held that position from 1768 to Oct. 1775. It is recorded that in 1803, when eighty-six years old, he was one of the Justices. A brother was one of the victims of the prison-ship cruelties during the Revolution. Comfort Sage (a relative) it is said commanded a company of light-horse at the battle of Lexington, 1775.

Ebenezer Sage, son of David and father of John, was born in Chatham, 1755. He graduated from Yale College, 1788, in the same class with Joel Barlow and Noah Webster. He was a physician, and in 1784 settled in East-Hampton, N. Y. He was a skillful doctor and a gentleman of scholarly attainments. He was of the Jefferson school of politics, and was Member of Congress from Suffolk Co.,

N. Y., from 1809-1817, also a delegate to the Convention, 1821, for amending the Constitution of the State of New-York. He died in Sag-Harbor, N. Y., greatly lamented, 1835.

Ruth Smith, the daughter of Dr. William Smith, of South-ampton, N. Y., became the wife of Dr. Ebenezer Sage and the mother of John. She belonged to the family descend-ed from Richard Smith, who settled in Smithtown, Long Island, N. Y., 1663. This family is commonly known as the "Bull Smiths" and thus distinguished from the "Tan-gier Smiths."

Richard Smith was a Patentee of immense tracts of land both in New-York and Rhode Island. He was a soldier in Cromwell's wars, and the gun with which he fought and afterwards did good execution among the Indians, is a treasured relic in the family at the ancient homestead near Smithtown, where his grave and that of his wife still may be seen.

CHAPTER II.

John Sage was born in East-Hampton, N. Y., 1781. His parents lived on the quaint, shady street, in the house which Albert M. Payne modernized, and in which he now resides. He inherited sterling qualities of integrity, prudence and intelligence. These traits of character still distinguish persons of the same pedigree.

He did not remember the time when he could not read nor write, but never forgot how, when five years old, he was sent to "Dame Filer's" school. "Dame Filer" took little children (principally) to relieve their busy mothers, to to her house which stood 'till recently near the south end of the village. "Dame Filer" essayed to teach the rudiments. Her methods, or rather ways of so doing, left a strong and long impression upon this pupil, which in old age, when recalled to mind, afforded amusement to himself and hearers. Suffice it to say, the road to knowledge one hundred years ago was not enlivened as at the present day, by kindergartens or athletics. The Bible was often the text book from which was taught the alphabet, easy spelling and first reading lessons. Indeed, bible, birch and bench were the essential furniture of a school room, and did not make it a cheerful place for little Puritans.

When John was seven years old his father returned to Chatham, Ct., but after living there five years was induced to settle in Sag-Harbor, N. Y., and practice his profession. During the following five years John was a pupil at Clinton Academy, East-Hampton, N. Y. He was prepared at this school for Dartmouth College, which he entered in 1808, in his 18th year. He graduated, third in his class, and lived to see himself the last but one, who had not been "starred," as the Doctor expressed it. In old age he used to search the College catalogue to find a name of a college mate with an asterisk. It did not seem to be in any degree a depressing occupation, and when assured that he was the last living, but one other, of his class, would often repeat the fact to us children. It seemed to us, as perhaps to him, a position of dignified consideration.

Two letters written by the boy during the beginning of his college life, are by the changes and chances with which the whirligig of time often preserves and wields the destiny of inanimate objects, at my disposal. They were written to his father's friend, Mr. Henry Packer Dering. The first is dated :

DARTMOUTH COLLEGE, January, 1808.

DEAR SIR :

I am infinitely obliged to you for the favor you do me in franking my sister's letter. I should have written you last week but want of time must be my plea, and it was at the end of the term.

Vacation has now commenced, and of course now I am free from all exercises, but as there is a good library belonging to the College I shall never be out of business.

I saw by the papers which my father sent me the account of the death of Mr. Gelston ; this is a melancholy instance of the uncertainty of human life ; no one had better hopes of a long life than he could have, but fatal diversion put an end to his career.

The embargo which I hear has been laid on our ports is a strong measure ; but I suppose the Tories will not blame Mr. Jefferson for rashly plunging into war, when but just now they grumbled at his want of energy. Seemingly inconsistencies are easily reconciled by them ; let Mr. Jefferson do what he will, they without reason will always

dislike him.   Indeed their only reason amounts to no more
than this :

"I do not like thee, Dr. Fell,
The reason why I cannot tell,
But I don't like thee Dr. Fell."

I hardly know what to think of the present ministry of
England.   It is my opinion that they want to put off a war
with us 'till they can have time to equip the Danish fleet.
Perhaps the Tories who justified them in taking Copenha-
gen will see the fruits of that victory employed in burning
down their own houses.   They may then sing another
song.   It is very rarely that we can come across much
news, especially at this season of the year.   If anything
extraordinary happens in Canada we shall soon hear of it
here.   Adieu.   To your family present the compliments of
your humble servant,

JOHN S. SAGE.

David Gelston, while hunting deer on Gardiner's Island,
in company with the proprietor of the island, Mr. Henry
P. Dering, Capt. David Hand and others from Sag-Harbor,
was accidently shot by Capt. Hand.   The hunters were or-
dered to stand still, but this young man moved and there-
by received a death wound.   He was son or nephew of Mr.
David Gelston, who was Collector of the port of New-York,
and after whom he was named.

The second letter is extremely interesting after the lapse
of eighty-nine years, and such a vivid description of the
faculty of Dartmouth College at that early date, written
by one of its students, must be rare in its annals.

It is dated :

DARTMOUTH COLLEGE, April 2d, 1808.
DEAR SIR:

I gave you in my last some account of our President,
and now to complete the picture, I will say a few words
concerning the other members of the Government.

Our eldest Professor is John Smith, D. D., Prof. of Latin,

Greek, Hebrew and the Oriental tongues. He is a man of very tenacious memory, and blessed with a considerable show of application, which qualities are the only requisites to obtain a knowledge of the tongues. He is perfect master of Latin and Greek, which are his hobby-horses, but when he gets into the pulpit he sinks into nothing. He is never properly in his element unless at *hic, hac, hoc.* He is a miserable composuist, and indeed miserable at everything except the languages; he is very jealous of his dignity, and is continually lecturing the class for some fault in that respect; he is a rank Fed. and when he gets upon politics talks more like a mad man than anything else; he is in continual fear of Bonaparte, and already imagines the French bayonets at his side; and finally, to say the least, he is a perfect ignoramus in everything except what relates immediately to the languages. His Latin grammar is the best extant, and has been much approved of in Europe as the most useful work of the kind ever published. So much for Prof. Smith.

Dr. Nathan Smith, Prof. of Chemistry and Medicine, is perhaps the most skillful man in his profession of any in the U. S. He is the most active man I ever saw; he rides continually, allows himself scarcely any time to sleep, and perhaps his practice is the most extensive of any in the U. S. He has risen to his present eminence mainly by his own exertions; he never received a liberal education, and what learning he has he picked up himself. His profits are immense, and were he as frugal as the President of the College he might be as wealthy as any man in the U. S.

John Hubbard, Prof. of Natural Philosophy and Mathematics, is the most amiable of all the College Government. There is no man in this country who possesses so great a knowledge of philosophy. His knowledge is most of it picked up from his own observations, for he never lets any phenomenon pass by him without explaining it if possible. He is rather deficient in mathematics, but he posesses the most geographical knowledge of any man I ever saw. He was a soldier during the Revolution, and was I believe in almost every battle that took place,

Our last Prof. is Rosuelf Shirtleff, Prof. of Theology. He is talked of for President, but if the present President can prevent his stepping into his shoes he will do it. They have been at variance ever since Shirtleff was chosen, and the only reason for it is because Shirtleff is rather independent. He won't submit to everything the President says, as Profs. Smith and Hubbard will, but asserts his own opinion sometimes. Shirtleff is in principle a Hopkintonian. He has the strongest reasoning powers that I most ever saw, but has a very bad delivery. He is pretty austere, and if he ever should be president a new leaf would be turned over.

Upon the whole, sir, take our government together, there is not another to be compared to it in the U. S. There is not one which is so much respected by the students, and though they are very wild here, and backward to punish, there is not another College where there are so few capers cut or faults committed.

I am yours sincerely,

JOHN S. SAGE.

His early years were passed in the quiet village of Sag-Harbor, N. Y., but the political agitations of the period pervaded hamlets as well as cities. The spirit of the American Revolution tempered the ideas of men with as keen a ring of patriotism as the blades of their swords had sounded in the clash of victory. They had not yet grown rusty in the scabbard and were familiar objects in the household.

Primitive methods of travel prevented political leaders from massing their followers, or indeed having any headquarters, and the day of Clubs and Leagues had not dawned.

Honorable Ebenezer Sage lived in the house, still standing, at the rear of the Masonic Hall, in Sag-Harbor, N. Y. It was built by him, and much of the furniture he made

with his own hands, as he was very fond of amusing himself with carpenter's tools, also rather proud of having his
house furnished in the simplest manner, which he judged
to be in accordance with life in a young Republic.

Men who were participants in National affairs gathered
by the hospitable fireside, such as:

Thomas Dering, of Shelter Island, N. Y., a member of
the Provincial Convention, 1775, also the convention in
1777, for the purpose of forming the constitution of the
State of New-York; Ezra L'Hommedieu, who had been a
member of the Continental Congress and (with Thomas
Dering) was elected to the same convention in 1777; Jonathan Havens, a member of some of the early Congresses,
also of the convention in 1783, which adopted the Constitution of the United States; Rev. Lyman Beecher, who
lived in East-Hampton, N. Y., and was an orator and divine who was fond of displaying his intellectual ability of
hurling into the midst of this coterie as well as from the
pulpit, metaphysical propositions with powerful theological dexterity. (Without doubt, Priest Buell, his predeces-
sor, who lived in East-Hampton during the exciting times
of the Revolution, laid his hand in baptism and blessing
on the head of John when an infant.)

General Sylvester Dering, of Shelter Island, N. Y., who
was noted for tender piety and patriotic fidelity; he was a
member of the State Assembly and served for the interests
of Suffolk County; Henry Packer Dering, brother of Sylvester, who was appointed Collector of the port of Sag-
Harbor by Gen. Washington; (Sylvester and Henry were
sons of Thomas Dering); Dr. Abel Huntington, of East-
Hampton, N. Y., a member of Congress; Abraham Rose,
of Bridge-Hampton, and others, with names of estimation,
were the associates of his father.

Intercourse with such men influenced the young mind of John Sage, which retained the impress so given, that in mature life his society was sought by persons of high position in State affairs, who listened with the keenest appreciation to interesting, pithy and truthful assertions regarding events and schemes of the days of Jefferson, Madison, Burr and cotemporaries.

The following incident of school days the Doctor often told to the boys and girls of our family, and we children thought it so good that we called it "The Bell Story."

Clinton Academy is one of the oldest in the State of New York. It was founded 1784, and named in honor of George Clinton, Governor of the State. During his second term he presented the bell, and for this purpose visited East-Hampton. The occasion was one of celebration and Gov. Clinton was entertained with much ceremony by East-Hampton people. The Doctor related the story in the following style :

THE BELL STORY.

"I remember the Governor's visit to East-Hampton. It made a great stir in the town, and as the Academy was the first place at which he was to present himself, of course it was there that the people congregated. I was a very absent-minded boy of twelve or thirteen years of age. My skin was very white and I well remember the freckles. My hair was red, my eyes dark brown, so you see that I was not a pretty boy. The teachers assiduously, but ineffectually, tried to induce me to dress up, so that by my personal appearance I might express a due respect for his 'Excellency.' The boys were ordered to be in line on the street in front of the Academy, and everybody was awaiting the great arrival which was to be heralded by the blowing of a horn as the stage entered Buell's Lane.

"Seeing my comrades dressed in their best clothes

caused me to reflect, and I decided that I ought in some fashion to acknowledge the demands of the day. I was barefooted, as we boys generally were week days during the summer, (always on Town Meeting day in the spring boys were allowed to go without their shoes and stockings) and in a spirit of enthusiasm off I ran to the town pump and showered my feet under the spout. *I have ever since regretted this act*, because I made myself more conspicuous by their whiteness, and the boys set up such a laugh ; yes, and some girls.

"The stage horn sounded, the bell rung, and the stage came into view at the turning of the lane into the street; the scholars waved their caps and hurrahed! hurrahed! hurrahed! After this a boy stepped forward and pronounced an address of welcome to the Governor. Colonel Samuel Huntting was the proud orator. He was a handsome boy, and he did it admirably.

"We had to be very respectful to our elders. Boys were fined for not raising their caps to the teachers, and parents were fined if we were seen on the street after nine o'clock at night."

Mrs. Lyman Beecher, the mother of Henry Ward Beecher and Harriet Beecher Stowe, had a boarding School for young ladies in East-Hampton, N. Y. Fanny Sage, John's only sister, was one of the pupils. They were taught the accomplishments then fashionable, and in painting and embroidery a degree of excellence was attained quite equal to that of the present day. Samples of exquisite needlework done by some of these girls are occasionally to be seen in the homes of descendants. The subjects often were classical, such as "Hector's Parting with Andromache." The stitches of various colored silks give the effect of painting on black or white satin. The date, with name and age of worker, preserved under glass, in a frame of antique device, adds to the interest of these treasured heirlooms. Mrs. Beecher painted miniatures, and she was a lady of superior mind and graces. (See an account of this school in Autobiography of Dr. Lyman Beecher, London, 1863, Chap. 22, Vol. I.

EXTRACTS FROM A MANUSCRIPT ACCOUNT OF THE OPENING OF CLINTON ACADEMY.

"The Academy was opened January, 1785. The exercises began with psalmody suited to the occasion, which was followed with prayer and sermon by Rev. Dr. Buell, from Acts vii, 22.

"Miss Fanny Rysam,* with more than usual elegance, pronounced 'The Messiah,' by Mr. Pope, and was succeeded by Mr. John Gardiner, who with a dignity of eloquence superior to his age pronounced the following oration."

We cannot give the oration, as it is too lengthy, but copy some of his expressions in regard to the improved accommodations :

"The house in which we are now met is by far the most elegant that many of us have ever seen."

"The apartments to which we are this day introduced are every way calculated for our delight, our comfort, our convenience."

"To be thus accommodated, you must be sensible, is greatly to our advantage, yet they are but outlines of that attention which is to be bestowed on our education."

"Now say, my ingenuous mates, what are your feelings who have heretofore thought it a precious opportunity to get but one month's schooling in our little dark forsaken cell ?"

As he looks forward he sees going forth from the institution "the dexterous clerk, the competent accountant, the renowned orator, the eminent physician, the judicious statesman, the venerable divine, and with them the accomplished *fair* to give society its highest tastes."

This oration was written on between three and four

---

* My grandmother.

sheets of foolscap, and after speaking of the Revolutionary struggle which was recently passed, giving due honor to Otis, Franklin and Adams, not forgetting the "Age of Reason," he closed with appropriate addresses to his schoolmates and to the citizens through whose efforts the institution was founded.

The prophecies of John Gardiner have been fulfiled. Many who have occupied honorable positions in mercantile, professional, political and literary careers were pupils at Clinton Academy. Among the "accomplished fair" are ladies who have graced society's highest circles.

One of the teachers was the father of John H. Payne, the author of "Home, Sweet Home," whose childhood was passed in this peaceful village, and no doubt impressed his mind with the spirit of that world-wide known song.

This digression is made because of the connection of John Sage's boyhood with Clinton Academy. The building is still standing and visited with interest by sojourners in this summer retreat.

CHAPTER III

MANHOOD.

After graduating from Dartmouth, Sage studied medicine with his father; also in the city of New-York. At this date colleges where the study of theology, medicine and law could be pursued, as now, were unknown in America. It was the custom for a person desiring one of these professions to study with some one of these callings, pass an examination, and receive a license to practice or follow the vocation of a minister.

John Sage was a close student of mathematical tastes. His vigorous mind did not shrink from solitary research in science, while love for his mother seemed to satisfy his heart's desires.

At this period his father was considered with the highest esteem throughout Suffolk County, N. Y., and Congressional life in Washington made him known to various persons of distinction. He desired his son to accept some position more advantageous for his abilities than available in a retired and almost isolated locality like the eastern part of Long Island at that date. He wanted him to have a political career. He was exceedingly displeased and deeply regretted that the young man declined the position of private secretary to Gallatin, then our minister to the Court of France. He had given him the best advantages of education to be obtained in America.

Though John was eccentric in manners, yet a talent for humor, brilliant and instructive conversational capacity made the young man a most agreeable companion.

His scientific and literary tastes were within the range

of mathematics, chemistry and languages; but such was his retiring disposition, bashfulness, and sensitiveness to public opinion, that the combination in temperament amounted almost to an affliction. His friends were indignant at his scorn of the "pomps and vanities," and still more at the extreme shyness of fellow beings.

Dr. Sage said that a crowd was a *bete noir* always for him. How different might have been his life and renowned his reputation if he had not chosen to be a recluse.

His sister, Fanny Sage, married Dr. Lawton and settled in Mobile, Ala., and Dr. Sage, influenced by this circumstance, went there to begin the practice of medicine. Strange to say, it was very distasteful to him, but the study of the healing art was the charm. Profound thought, caution and skill were the marked characteristics of the practitioner.

His experience in Mobile was very sad. Mrs. Lawton and her husband took the yellow fever, from which they died. Dr. Sage also had it, but when sufficiently recovered returned to his father's house in Sag-Harbor, N. Y. For months his health in consequence suffered. When able to walk the short distance between the house and that of the intimate neighbor, Henry P. Dering, (now the Douglass house on Union street) he was obliged to support himself step by step by holding to the fence.

When he became better he aided his father for awhile in the care of the sick. Subsequently he spent quite a period of time in New-York, Philadelphia and other cities.

He took a voyage to the Isle of France, where the romance of Paul and Virginia was laid, and he always enjoyed recalling the scenes of the visit to this beautiful isle. In these sojourns a knowledge of the world was gained and his character became more reliant.

A serious love affair in New-York, with a southern lady, which unfortunately proved "that the course of true love *does not* run smooth," (sometimes) was the only one which ever came to light. He was not "a ladies' man," yet ladies enjoyed his society and felt honored and flattered by any attention from him. Once in extreme old age, when bantered as to his bachelorhood, he replied in a light hearted manner, "I once had a deary." It was a surprise, and the thought came to mind:

"The past is not, but memory gives
Her brightest hues to days gone by."

When asked why he never married, the usual reply was: "It is not in my power to make a woman happy, and surely I do not wish to make any woman unhappy." As to the popular opinion that a physician was more sought after when a married man, he said: "that is a fallacy not worth disputing when compared with real professional merit."

Dr. Sage believed that most sickness was the result of a fault or imprudence regarding general laws of health, because of the prevailing ignorance of these laws. Otherwise folly and accidents were the causes. Among his opinions the following come to mind:

"Most drugs effect more harm than good."

"Most ailments could be alleviated, and in many cases cured, by diet and rest."

"Each person has his own degree of temperature for comfort: sixty degrees for one, eighty for another. Nothing is more irritating than arbitrary methods in this matter."

"The fear of pain should not be encouraged. Bodily pain and mental suffering were for the good of humanity and a guide to the physician in his diagnosis."

Anesthetics and narcotics were only to be used in extreme cases, and their frequent use, as at the present day, deeply deplored.

"Never disregard the crying of a child. Try at once to make it comfortable. Care for its body and govern its temper."

He thought that the preparation of medical prescriptions was a part of a physician's duties, and should be of his medical education. The few remedies that he used were compounded with care by himself. He said, "Pharmacy would not have attained so lucrative a place in business, if doctors had continued the old fashioned way of making pills, powders, salves, jalaps and drops.

Dr. Sage was very fond of music, and played the violin with grace and skill. He was an accomplished whistler. He was familiar with the operas and dramas of the day, and when in the city frequented the opera house and the theatre. He was a superior whist player. When opportunity offered he liked to listen to ministers of repute. The Presbyterian Church was his choice, however his mind was well stored with knowledge of different forms of religions and with bible truths.

In the village home only his intimates suspected or knew of these traits. Here he studied, composed, translated and experimented, and within the rich resources of his mind found employment.

In conversation he excelled and in company he was the leading man. His personal appearance inspired respect and deference. He was a tall man of large frame, well proportioned.

With intimate friends he was often absent-minded, and Mrs. William R. Sleight relates, that one evening, when at her father's house, (H. P. Dering) with her young brothers and sisters, he withdrew from the genial group into a corner and for an hour watched the flame of a candle which he held. None of the company thought of interfering or criticising, for they knew that some scientific puzzle was being investigated. "It was one of John's ways."

This lady also tells that he undertook to construct a balloon. Her brother Thomas was taken into his confidence and aided him. The lower story of the old Arsenal, which stood on Union street, near the Presbyterian Church, was used for the workshop. He made various instruments for mathematical measurements, such as barometer, thermometer, and time-keeper. These were of his own invention. Books were not as common as now, especially translations, and he translated for friends stories from Latin and French writers.

He loved to impart knowledge, but not display his inventions. We children, with whom he was associated, can never forget how gracious was his manner when he helped us sometimes with our lessons. Not anything like the pedant scared us, and names might be mentioned of men and women who have told us that to Dr. Sage they owe a debt of gratitude for their culture in literature.

The mathematics of LePlace he studied in the French, and discovered and corrected some errors of calculation, which were shown and proved to a few who were able to comprehend the work.

A gentleman told me that an intricate account involving a large sum of money connected with the settlement of a whaling voyage caused much disagreement, and it seemed necessary that an expert accountant would have to be employed to adjust it. Some one suggested that it be shown to Dr. Sage. This was done, and in an incredibly short time the computations were made correct and satisfactory to all concerned. The Doctor would not receive any remuneration, saying it was a simple matter to him and gave him great pleasure to be of any assistance. Otherwise it would have cost a good deal and involved perhaps a lawsuit.

A LETTER.

In concluding this chapter we give the following interesting letter regarding Doctor Sage from Judge Charles P. Daly, President of the American Geographical Society:

MISS MULFORD.

You no doubt know that there was a period in the world's history when the icy region of the Arctic had a warm climate, equivalent to that of South Carolina, as is attested by the fossil remains of large trees that grew there, specimens of the trunks of which are to be seen in European museums. Trees still grow there and attain considerable age, but so very small that Dr. Hays told me that he could cover a forest of them with his hat.

Since the discovery that the Arctic had once a warm climate, some six or seven theories have been advanced by scientific men, to account for a state of things there in the past which now seems so extraordinary, among whom was an English Colonel of scientific attainments, who wrote a book to establish that a warm climate formerly in the Arctic was owing to what is known as the Precession of the Equinoxes, a slow, continual change of the position of the earth toward the sun, from east to west; a spiral movement which occupies about 25,000 years, and this movement, which has been known from the time of the Greeks, he undertook to establish by a series of astronomical calculations founded upon observations, brought the Arctic at one period of this spiral rotation, so directly under the sun's rays and heat as to give it the warm climate which undoubtedly it formerly possessed.

Being interested in the subject I got the book, and after reading it I thought if the theory were probable, if all the computations and facts stated in it were correct, of which I was not competent to judge and knowing that Dr. Sage was not only a profound mathematician but a man of extensive astronomical knowledge, I sent the book to him to know what he should say to it, and the following day he returned it, with a memorandum stating that some of the computations were numerically incorrect; that others were founded upon conjectural observation that astronomically were of no value, as the instruments did not then exist by which accurate observations could be made, and that the book therein did not prove anything.

That he should have come to this conclusion was not in itself remarkable, but that he should within twenty-four hours have not only read the book, which was a good-sized duodecimo, but have mastered it going over all its computations and testing all its astronomical statements, shows what a mathematician he was and how thorough his knowledge of astronomy.

I once told him that he was the first person I had met who had read LaPlace's Mecanique Celeste entirely through and his answer was: "that was a pleasure to be enjoyed but once."

I took Baron Osten Sacken, the Russian Charge, and afterwards the Russian Consul General in New-York, and a distinguished entomologist, who was visiting me, to see the Doctor, and he was struck as I have been, with his intellectual appearance and lofty forehead, for he was in appearance more like Baron Alexander Humbolt than any man I have ever seen. Baron Osten Sacken had a long and interesting conversation with him and when he came away said: "I was never more surprised than to find such a looking man with such acquirements in a little place like this, where you say, or its vicinity, he has passed his whole life. The place where you would expect to see such a man would be in the Prussian Senate."

Very truly yours,
CHAS. P. DALY,
North Haven.

Sept. 1896.

CHAPTER IV.

DECLINING DAYS.

When about sixty years old Doctor Sage gave up the active practice of medicine and zealously sought seclusion to enjoy study and repose. He built for himself a small house of his own peculiar plan, on the street at the rear of the Presbyterian Church, at that time a quiet by-street. His laboratory, sleeping room, library and "living room," were arranged as to be convenient, just for his own comfort. He was the last of his family. His nearest relatives, the Spencers and Seldens, from Middletown, Ct., made yearly visits, which were mutually enjoyed.

Old friendships were not relinquished, and when the Doctor made a call by the fireside of those who had been friends for years his hearty laugh and reminiscenses made the visit very welcome. If his strongest attachments were for men, he confessed to enjoying ladies' society. His manners were of the olden times and very courteous.

Among those with whom he was accustomed to visit informally and socially might be mentioned the families of Sleights, Hunttings, Derings, Mrs. John Fordham, Mr. John Sherry, Mulfords, Nicolls, Gardiners and L'Hommedieu. Among the last occasions at which he appeared in society was at the marriage of Miss Mary Sherry to Col. Peter French. There was dancing at the wedding. The Doctor was watching and probably comparing the modern style with that of former days, when Mrs. Dering asked: "Well, Doctor, what do you think of it?" He gravely replied: "It looks like a very serious affair."

Without doubt he was on the most intimate terms in the

Dering family. After the death of his father, which left the hearth desolate, while continuing to live in the old home until breaking up, he took his meals with the Derings. In 1840 Lodowick Dering, a son of H. P. Dering, married Eliza Gracie Mulford. Her family and the Doctor were old friends as well as that of her husband. When the young couple went to housekeeping in the house on Hampton street, where Mrs. Dering always lived, the three took the first meal together, and for forty-four years Doctor was the daily companion at the table.

Until about 1870, when infirmities began to prevent at times, no matter what the weather, he went to and fro from his house ; and so exact the path and methodical the hour, that one could safety regulate a watch at 8, 12 and 6 o'clock as the aged man passed for breakfast, dinner and supper. This long intercourse was without one episode of discord. It resembled that between father and daughter, and reminds one of the long friendship and solicitude of Mrs. Unwin for the poet Cowper. It was like what Emerson meant by—

"Happy the house that shelters a friend !"

also—

"The elements of friendship are truth and tenderness !"

We children saw its beautiful existence, and it is with a kind of emotion of reverence that any details are related.

Mrs. Dering's qualities of mind and person could entice a student from books and charm a recluse into a genial and entertaining companion. Her thorough belief in the Doctor's superiority of knowledge, and assuming the humble attitude of pupil, won his confidence so that he would often think aloud in her presence.

Thus it was that many a scientific matter which is yet not known or undeveloped was unfolded to her. Her real and often pretended ignorance of obtruse subjects, united

with witty and whimsical comments, gave the pleasure like
that Mozart enjoyed when explaining musical composition
to his unmusical housekeeper.

After three-score and ten years old Dr. Sage deliberately
burnt up the greater part of his written calculation and
translations. This deed destroyed works on mathematics,
chemistry, astronomy and languages. When remonstrated
with and the loss lamented, he replied : "When the time
that they are wanted comes someone will find out for themselves."

THE FIRE.

One morning the bachelor home took fire and burned
down. It was thought that its solitary occupant would
mourn it as a great loss. He was about eighty-five years
old. He refused to leave the blazing house until he got
ready, saying, "I know what I am about." With wonderful composure he directed the work of saving what was
possible, and from time to time would feel of the hot walls
in order to judge how much longer it was wise to tarry.
The crowd outside said, "The old man won't come out ; he
means to burn up." Mrs. Dering had come and repeated-
ly warned him of danger ; at last, covered with the ancient
looking camlet cloak, with velvet collar and silver clasp,
the broad brimmed hat on his head, the Doctor with the
faithful friend appeared.

Through the throng, assembled as usual on such occasions, and to whom the venerable man was looked upon
with curiosity or regard, they walked, silently, dignified,
to her house, apparently not affected by the circumstance
of a little house being destroyed. At noon his dinner was
heartily eaten and the matter treated as an accident liable
to happen "in the course of human events."

The following seven years this was his home. Early in
married life Mrs. Dering had become a widow, with two

sons. These boys grew to manhood, while their mother
seemed still to the Doctor's eyes the cheery, girlish companion as of old. This role was from habit unconsciously
sustained while striving to make these days happy.

His faculties were unimpaired until about eighty-nine
years old, when failing memory as to recent events, and
frequent hallucinations, made the hours weary for him and
anxious for her.

There is a French proverb, "That without woman the
two extremities of life would be devoid of succor, and the
middle of pleasure." It seemed as if Sage had somewhat
boasted of being independent of the latter clause, but in
youth and in age a mother and friend contributed to his
comfort. The clever and witty tricks to which Mrs. D. resorted when making believe to fall in with his hallucinations and gently leading the feeble mind back to reality
was a trial and strain to nerves, only comprehended by
those who have had a like experience. We will try to describe one or two of these occurrences just to show the resources of this charming lady on such occasions.

The Doctor became so childish that he did not like to
be alone, except for a few moments at a time, but constant-
ly followed Mrs. Dering or was seeking her. One evening
they were sitting by the fireside. The Doctor wore his hat
and seemed to be in deep meditation, while Mrs. Dering
was busy knitting. The time was silently and peacefully
prssing when three friends called. They were asked to sit
in the hall, just by the open door. In this way she could
enjoy the "running in" of neices and neighbors, without
disturbing the reveries of the Doctor, who had become
quite blind and deaf. They were spectators to the following off-hand drama. During a social converse with the
visitors, Doctor slowly turned toward her and said :

"Liizy, where are we now?"

This remark sounded like delirium, but equally so did her immediate reply :

"Why, Doctor, we're aground."

"Oh," was his placid comment, and he arranged his position to a poise as of one sailing when becalmed and the boat gets aground, and there is nothing to do but wait patiently for a breeze.

Conversation was resumed without an allusion to the side act. At the end of about a quarter of an hour Doctor began to look leisurely around the room, and remarks :

"Liizy, our accommodations are very comfortable in this packet." (This word packet for sloop is obsolete.)

Falling again into the hallucination she at once replied : "Yes ; those bunks look very clean. It is tedious being becalmed, but we shall get off soon, for there comes a puff of wind."

Doctor thought they were sailing across the sound from New London to Sag-Harbor. He was living over some bygone day. Gradually and tenderly he was led to imagine that the wind had changed and was floating them into port.

Another time, during a blinding snow storm, after dark, he had an hallucination that he was about to start from Brooklyn by stage for home, as fifty years previous was the way to travel. To have opposed him would have aroused a fury more dangerous with the mental feebleness than exposure to the storm. He insisted upon going out of doors and she was puzzled how to manage the case. Soon the bright eyes beamed with a brilliant idea; at least it was an expedient. Calling a maid to her assistance she said :

"Show this gentleman to the stage. It storms so against the front door that he must go out of the back door, around the house to the front gate, where the stage is waiting."

Doctor followed the maid, and after floundering in the snow his brain became cooler than his body and the hallucination vanished. In the meantime she hastened to the front door, ready to act the part of welcoming a traveller, but it was not necessary.

Realizing the situation and the artifice, he praised her quick wit, laughed at the ruse, but pitifully lamented the necessity, saying :

"I never thought that my mind would fail before my body. That was an illusion."

Contrary to the usual manner of old age he did not lose interest in current topics. When told of inventions and discoveries he did not doubt nor ridicule but was pleased with accurate descriptions. He would describe and foretell its possibilities and commonly remark, with animation : ' Indeed ! the deuce ! Well, if the fellows have found out that secret the world will be greatly benefitted."

He was very particular in business dealings and at this period would so often say to any one doing him a favor, no matter how trifling, "Allow me to recompense you," and perhaps recklessly hand a greenback or coin without any appreciation of its value, that it came into Mrs. Dering's mind to substitute some imitation bills in his pocket-book with which he could be lavish in generosity ; therefore she cut out of green tissue paper these imitation bills. He found them in his vest pocket but they did not answer the purpose very long. Afrer a day of feeling and scrutinizing the paper he came to Mrs. D. with one in his hand and said, "Liizy, this is not money ; what have you been doing? You are very smart, but I am too much for you, I am afraid."

Often by himself, he was fond of repeating long passages from the poets, and well do we remember hearing page after page from Hudibras, and the hearty laugh at the satire, just as if it was a recent production.

Thus declining days were brightened until the weary one was relieved of the burden of his earthly life. Dr. John Sage died in 1882, in his ninety-third year.

The cessation of the companionship, friendship and solicitude which had existed for so long a time as forty-four years made a void in the life of Eliza Gracie Dering. Her sons had gone into world for business, one in Chicago and one in Philadelphia, and the occupation of watching the steps and cheering the hours of her charge had passed. Friends noticed that she began "to fail and age."

About four years after the death of Dr. Sage, one Sunday evening while the purple, scarlet and gold of a June sunset colored the sky with opaline tints and the hushed air of twilight was tremulous with chimes of church bells, watchers saw a love-glow spread over her face. Was it the reflection of the clestial light in realms of bliss as angelic music from the choir invisible welcomed her spirit when it entered the Eternal City? We who had tenderly cared for her during a short illness said : "She is dead."

THE END.

APPENDIX.

Cooper the Novelist and Dr. Ebenezer Sage.

——:o:——

THE SEA LIONS, the last but one of Cooper's thirty-three novels, and one among his best, begins with an account of Sag-Harbor as it was in 1819 and 1820. It is not a description drawn from the novelist's imagination, but from actual observation, for Cooper at that period was temporarily a resident there. He had resigned from the navy and had married a lady named Delancy, from Westchester Co., N. Y., who was a connection of the Nicoll's family, of Shelter Island, N. Y. While on a visit to this family and in company with Charles T. Dering, a shipping merchant of Sag-Harbor and the husband of Miss Eliza Floyd Nicoll, his attention was drawn to the whale fishery, Sag-Harbor being then one of the principal whaling ports of the country, with a population in 1820 of 1,646, nearly half of what it is now. He became so much interested in this industry, and being then without any pursuit or occupation, he resolved to engage in that business and purchased a ship in which he had the controlling interest, called the Union, commanded by Capt. Jonathan Osborne, of Wainscott, one of the most noted of the whaling captains that sailed then from Sag-Harbor. Judge Hedges, in his recent History of East-Hampton, N. Y.* in referring to Captain Osborne, says : "he had sailed from Sag-Harbor on voyages in command of a ship from thence, owned by J. Fennimore Cooper, the novelist," from which it might be inferred that the vessel was owned by Cooper, but it appears from infor-

---

*Hedges' History of East-Hampton, p. 178, Sag-Harbor, 1897.

mation derived from old residents who are familiar with
the facts that Cooper and O. T. Dering, the husband of his
wife's cousin, formed a company composed of several persons, the controlling interest in which vessel, as has been
said, belonged to the novelist.

The Judge gives a vivid description of the capture of a
whale off East-Hampton by two boats led by this famous Captain Osborne, a contest which lasted from seven in
the morning until two in the afternoon, which he witnessed
as a boy seventy years ago from his father's farm. He
describes the victors "towing the whale to the shore, the
joyful faces of the crew, the tall and stalwart form of the
Captain clad in his red flannel shirt, his face and hands
almost equally red," looking "the incarnation of the whale
fighter fame had reported him to be," and the Judge adds,
Cooper's "creation of Long Tom Coffin out of Capt. Jonathan Osborne would be a slight dilation of the reality."

Cooper, as being the largest shareholder, took charge on
behalf of the others of whatever was incidental to the "fitting out" of the vessel and the general management of the
business. It is said he was the first to originate, at least
in Sag-Harbor, the scheme of an association of several persons who united in purchasing and sending out a vessel on
a whaling voyage, or what was thereafter called "company
ships." Whaling vessels before this time, in that port, being owned either by an individual or a business firm.

While in Sag-Harbor engaged in this business Cooper
resided in a tavern at the bottom of Main street, near the
site of the present Railroad depot, a noted place of resort
in the early part of the present century, kept by one Peletiah Fordham, who from his personal peculiarities and self
importance, was known by the sobrequet of "Duke Fordham." Here, according to a tradition that has descended

both from the Nicolls and Dering families,* Cooper wrote his first novel, "Precaution," which may have been, for he was residing in Sag-Harbor when the novel was published, in 1819, that being the year when the Union, under his business management, sailed upon a voyage to the coast of Brazil, which at that time was the part of the South Seas chiefly resorted to by whalers, and having, both before and after her departure much leisure, it may have been that he sought to fill it up by the writing of this work, which was not written with any serious expectation then of devoting himself to a literary career.

It is said that after reading a recent English novel called Discipline, which he brought from New-York, aloud to his wife and her cousin, Miss Anne Nicoll, he remarked that he could write a better novel himself. The ladies expressed their doubt. They, and especially Miss Nicoll, challenged him to do so, and Precaution was written to prove it, which it did not, as the novel was unsuccessful.

Judge Hedges in an interesting paper, recently read before the Sag-Harbor Historical Society, after stating that he was told by a person who knew the fact, that Cooper stopped at Peletiah Fordham's tavern, on Main street, adds this respecting the tradition that it was in that tavern that he wrote his first novel, Precaution. "Strangely and lately there came into my hands a copy of a letter written by his daughter, the late Susan Fennimore Cooper, dated January 7th, 1891, to the Rev. William Remson Mulford, of New Haven, in which she states that at the time the novel was written her father resided at Angevine, Westchester County, N. Y., and when a child she heard him read the manuscript to her mother, which was written there."

* See also note by Wm. S. Pelletreau in the Records of Southampton, Vol. III, p. 246.

This does not necessarily disprove the statement that it was written in Fordham's tavern, in Sag-Harbor. The circumstance which led to its being written occurred at the residence of his wife's cousin, Miss Anne Nicoll, on Shelter Island ; the anecdote having been frequently told by her both before and after Cooper became famous.

Precaution was published in 1819, and in the summer of that year the Union returned from her first voyage, under Cooper's superintendence, to Sag-Harbor, and was again fitted out for another whaling voyage, under the same master, from which she returned in the summer of the following year. During these three years Cooper, in the discharge of the duties he had undertaken, must have, as the manager of this whaling adventure, passed a considerable portion of his time in Sag-Harbor, especially during the fitting out for these two cruises, and the business attendant upon the disposition of the cargoes she brought back, which would make him temporarily a resident there, while his permanent residence or home may have been in Westchester County, N. Y., where he married his wife.

It is stated that when Mrs. Cooper was in the eastern part of Long Island, it was either as the guest of her relatives, in the Nicoll mansion on Shelter Island, or with her cousin, Mrs. Charles T. Dering, in Sag-Harbor, the residue of her time probably being passed at the permanent residence or home in Westchester County, so that it may have been that this first novel was written at Fordham's tavern in Sag-Harbor, and that Cooper brought the manuscript to his residence at Angevine to read it to his wife. If Miss Cooper had heard, either from her father or her mother, that the novel was written at Angevine, it would have a weight, which merely saying "which was written there" has not. She was at the time a child, and as her parents had been married but a few years, a young child, and her saying "which was written there" may have been simply her impression and belief, from having heard her father read it there, from the manuscript, to her mother.

As the circumstance that led to its being written occurred at Shelter Island, and as the business he had to do in Sag-Harbor left him with much leisure on his hands, it would seem very natural, after the challenge he had received, that he should at once, having the leisure to do so, have set about doing what he declared he could do, and that the novel was written at Fordham's tavern, according to tradition, which from inquiries made by the writer has existed there for a long time, and believed, and that when completed he brought the manuscript to his wife in West-chester County to read to her.

The Union returned from her voyage on the 15th of July, 1820, with 900 barrels of oil, the capture of twelve whales, about half a cargo for a vessel of her tonnage, which was not what was then considered a very good voyage.

Note.—Mrs. Mary Balfour Brunton was the wife of the Rev. Alexan - der Brunton and the authoress of two novels, "Self-Control" and "Discipline," which were very successful, especially the first, "Self-Control." It was published anonymously in 1811, and what is very unusual in any book, the first edition was sold in a month, and especially so in the case of a first publication by an unknown author; its second and third edition followed. It was written, as the authoress afterward stated, to show that the maxim is untrue that a reformed rake make the best husband. "Discipline," which was published in 1814, it is said, also met with great success. She left another novel, "Emmeline," unfinished at the time of her death, four years afterwards. Many of her writings have been translated into French, and she is said to have been highly esteemed on the continent, and that among the pleasing expounders of morality that she stood prominent as well for the good taste and style as for the soundness of her works.—(Alibone's Dictionary of Authors, Vol. I, p. 259.) The fact that her two novels were so successful, when she had as competitors, in the field of fiction, Miss Edgworth, Lady Morgan, Hannah More, Jane Austin and Sir Walter Scott, is a sufficient commentary on Cooper's want of appreciation of the last of her two novels, who did not justly esteem the merits of others, for after Scott's death he wrote an article upon him in a New-York magazine, in which all the merit he allowed him as a novelist was tact.

To illustrate what was, Captain David Vail of Sag-Harbor, in 1836, returned to that port in the Cadmus, the Havre packet ship that brought LaFayette to this country in 1824, as a guest of the nation, and afterwards became a whaling vessel owned by the shipping firm of Mulford & Sleight, of Sag-Harbor, which brought back after an absence of only seven months, 2,000 barrels of oil.

The Union made two successive voyages thereafter with Captain Osborne as master, to the coast of Patagonia, rereturning to Sag-Harbor respectively on the third of July, 1821, and the 24th of June, 1822, with what results has not been ascertained. If they had been largely profitable it may reasonably be surmised that Cooper would have continued in the business, and if the investment had not been much of a success that he would have availed himself of anything better and equally congenial that may have offered, and about this period something of the kind may have taken place. As respects that business he himself says in the Sea Lions, "None became rich in the strict signification of the term, though a few got to be in reasonably affluent circumstances ; many were placed altogether at their ease, and more were made humbly comfortable."

The Union continued to be employed in the whaling trade of Sag-Harbor for some years thereafter, but on her next voyage, which was in 1823, she was no longer commanded by Captain Osborne, but by a Captain Griffing, and about the same period an important event happened in respect to Cooper. It has been stated that the first novel he published was a failure ; that it had no success. Such however was not the case with the second. A person then living in the vicinity where Cooper had married his wife, named Enoch Crosby, had played an important part

in the American Revolution, in keeping Washington supplied with valuable information respecting the enemy, with
whose perilous adventures, many disguises and hair-breadth
escapes Cooper became acquainted, and considering this as
supplying excellent material for a work of fiction, he produced and published in 1821 his novel of The Spy, which
had a wide-spread popularity, was re-printed in England,
was translated into many languages, and established his
reputation as a successful writer of fiction.

It would seem that at or about this period he withdrew
from the whaling business, for the Union continued to be
employed for several years thereafter, commanded by different masters. There is a record in the Sag-Harbor Custom House of her return from a whaling voyage on the 16th
of June, 1827, but nothing indicating that he had any connection with her. He had in the intervening seven years
evidently devoted himself wholly to the pursuit of literature, having published during that time The Pioneers, The
Pilot, The Last of the Mohicans, (generally considered his
masterpiece), The Prairie, The Red Rover, and had become
one of the world's prominent novelists. Balsac admired
him greatly and Victor Hugo thought that as a writer of
romance, he was superior to Scott.

A small seaport town as Sag-Harbor was then, where the
whole industry of the place was connected with ships and
shipping, would necessarily bring together curious, excen-
tric and striking personages, of which a writer of fiction, to
aid him in portraying character, could avail himself, or,
as Cooper expresses it, use as "auxiliaries," and that he
did so is highly probable, at least in one case. He says :
"That the character of Leather Stocking is a creation rendered possible by such auxiliaries as were necessary to
produce the effect." The description of the personal ap-

pearance and peculiar laugh of Natty Bumpo, of the Pioneers, nicknamed Leather Stocking, was recognized at the time of the publication of the novel to be that of Captain Hand, of Sag-Harbor.

From the first part of the book we quote the following description of Natty Bumpo, which, in the recollection of persons now living, is an exact delineation of Capt. Hand's personality in old age* :

"His face was skinny and thin almost to emaciation ; but yet it bore no signs of disease ; on the contrary it had every indication of the most robust and enduring health. The cold and the exposure had, together, given it a color of uniform red. His gray eyes were glancing under a pair of shaggy brows, that overhung them in long hairs of gray mingled with their natural hue ; his scraggy neck was bare and burnt to the same tint as his face."

A few pages beyond we read that Leather Stocking laughed thus : " * * then Natty stretched out his long and bony neck and straightened his body, as he opened his mouth, which exposed a single tusk of yellow bone, while his eyes, his face, even his whole frame seemed to laugh, although no sound was emitted except a kind of hissing, as he inhaled his breath in quavers." This "remarkable laugh," as Cooper calls it, is identified throughout the Leather Stocking series.

Captain Hand, of whom mention elsewhere is made, was a seaman in privateers and vessels of the navy during the Revolution, and before reaching his 20th year had seen Washington, been a prisoner of war five times, and was one of the exchanged prisoners from the Jersey prison ships. He was distinguished by the further circumstance that he had five wives. These were interred in a row, each

* He was the maternal grandfather of the present Capt. David Vail, of Sag-Harbor.

with a headstone, in the old burying ground of the Presbyterian church in Sag-Harbor, at the end of the ground fac-
ing Madison St., where as he walked along the street he
could easily see the tombstones of his five wives, of which
at his death in 1840, at the age of 81, his was the sixth,
placed at the head of the row.   On the stone at the grave
of the third wife is this curious epitaph, probably of his
own composition :

> "Behold ye living mortals passing by,
>   How thick the partners of one husband lie ;
>   Vast and unsearchable are the ways of God,
>   Just but severe His chastening rod."

They have been removed to Oakland cemetery where they
are placed as formerly they were, in a row.   Howell, in his
History of Southampton, says of him: "Having survived
all the dangers of war, he lived long, a man of note and re-
spectability, honored by his fellow citizens for his bravery
and manly virtues."

There is this further interest in the Sea Lions that Dr.
Ebenezer Sage is one of the personages introduced in the
opening part of the tale, whose character, in the opinion of
persons still living, is faithfully delineated, and it was
thought that in addition to the early account given by
Cooper of Sag-Harbor it would be interesting in connection with the letters written by Dr. Ebenezer Sage in the
earlier part of this century, to reprint so much of Cooper's
novel as relates to him.

The novelist's description of Sag-Harbor and its vicinity,
and the habits, character and pursuits of the people of the
eastern end of Long Island, seventy-eight years ago, are so
interwoven that much of the opening part of the novel has
to be re-printed nearly entire.   The description opens as
follows :

Every one at all familiar with the map of America knows

the position and general form of the two islands that shelter the well-known harbor of the great emporium of the
commerce of the country. These islands obtained, their
names from the Dutch, who called them Nassau and Staten;
but the English, with little respect for the ancient house
whence the first of these appellations is derived, and consult-
ing only the homely taste which leads them to a practical
rather than to a poetical nomenclature in all things, have
since virtually dropped the name of Nassau, altogether sub-
stituting that of Long Island in its stead.

Long Island, or the island of Nassau, extends from the
mouth of the Hudson to the eastern line of Connecticut;
forming a sort of sea-wall to protect the whole coast of the
latter little territory against the waves of the broad Atlan-
tic. Three of the oldest New-York counties, as their names
would imply, Kings, Queens and Suffolk, are on this island.
Kings was originally peopled by the Dutch, and still possesses as many names derived from Holland as from England, if its towns, which are of recent origin, be taken from
the account. Queens is more of a mixture, having been
early invaded and occupied by adventurers from the other
side of the Sound; but Suffolk, which contains nearly, if
not quite, two-thirds of the surface of the whole Island, is
and ever has been in possession of a people derived originally from the Puritans of New England. Of these three
counties, Kings is much the smallest, though, next to New-
York itself, the most populous county in the State; a circumstance that is owing to the fact that two suburban off-
sets of the great emporium, Brooklyn and Williamsburg,
happen to stand within its limits, on the waters of what is
improperly called the East River; an arm of the sea that
has obtained this appellation in contradistinction to the
Hudson, which, as all Manhattanese well know, is as often
called the North River as by its proper name. In consequence of these two towns, or suburbs of New-York, one of
which contains nearly one hundred thousand souls, while
the other must be drawing on toward twenty thousand,
Kings County has lost all it ever had of peculiar or local
character. The same is true of Queens, though in a dimin-

ished degree; but Suffolk remains Suffolk still, and it is with Suffolk alone that our present legend requires us to deal. Of Suffolk, then, we propose to say a few words by way of preparatory explanation.

Although it has actually more sea-coast than all the rest of New-York united, Suffolk has but one seaport that is ever mentioned beyond the limits of the county itself. Nor is this port one of general commerce, its shipping being principally employed in the hardy and manly occupation of whaling. As a whaling town, Sag-Harbor is the third or fourth port in the country, and maintains something like that rank in importance. A whaling haven is nothing without a whaling community. Without the last it is almost hopeless to look for success. New-York can, and has often fitted whalers for sea, having sought officers in the regular whaling ports; but it has been seldom that the enterprises have been rewarded with such returns as to induce a second voyage by the same parties.

It is as indispensable that a whaler should possess a certain *esprit de corps*, as that a regiment, or a ship of war, should be animated by its proper spirit. In the whaling communities, this spirit exists to an extent and in a degree that is wonderful, when one remembers the great expansion of this particular branch of trade within the last five-and-twenty years. It may be a little lessened of late, but at the time of which we are writing, or about the year 1820, there was scarcely an individual who followed this particular calling out of the port of Sag-Harbor, whose general standing on board ship was not as well known to all the women and girls of the place as it was to his shipmates. Success in taking the whale was a thing that made itself felt in every fibre of the prosperity of the town; and it was just as natural that the single-minded population of that part of Suffolk should regard the bold and skilful harpooner or lancer with favor, as it is for the belle at a watering-place to bestow her smiles on one of the young heroes of Cottreras or Cherubusco. His peculiar merit, whether with the oar, lance, or harpoon, is bruited about, as well as the number of whales he may have succeeded in "making fast to," or those which he caused to "spout blood." It is true that the great extension of the trade within the last twenty years, by drawing so many from a distance into its pursuits, has in a degree lessened this local interest and local knowledge of character; but at the time of which we are about to write both were at their height, and Nantucket itself had not more of this "intelligence office" propensity, or more of the true whaling *esprit de corps*, than were to be found in the district of country that surrounded Sag-Harbor.

Long Island forks at its eastern end, and may be said to have two extremities. One of these, which is much the shortest of the two legs thus formed, goes by the name of Oyster Pond Point; while the other, that stretches much farther in the direction of Block Island, is the well-known cape called Montauk. Within the fork lies Shelter Island, so named from the snug berth it occupies. Between Shelter Island and the longest or southern prong of the fork are the waters which compose the haven of Sag-Harbor—an estuary of some extent; while a narrow but deep arm of the sea separates this island from the northern prong, that terminates at Oyster Pond.

The name of Oyster Pond Point was formerly applied to a long, low, fertile, and pleasant reach of land that extended several miles from the point itself, westward, toward the spot where the two prongs of the fork united. It was not easy, during the first quarter of the present century, to find a more secluded spot on the whole Island than Oyster Pond. Recent enterprises have since converted it into the terminus of a railroad; and Green Port, once called Sterling, is a name well known to travelers between New-York and Boston; but in the earlier part of the present century it seemed just as likely that the *Santa Casa* of Loretta should take a new flight and descend on the point, as that the improvement that has actually been made should in truth occur at that out-of-the-way place. It required, indeed, the keen eye of a railroad projector to bring this spot in connection with anything; nor could it be done without having recourse to the water by which it is almost surrounded. Using the last, it is true, means have been found to place it in a line between two of the great marts of the country, and thus to put an end to all its seclusion, its simplicity, its peculiarities, and we had almost said, its happiness.

It is to us ever a painful sight to see the rustic virtues rudely thrown aside by the intrusion of what are termed improvements. A railroad is certainly a capital invention for the traveller, but it may be questioned if it is of any other benefit than that of pecuniary convenience to the places through which it passes. How many delightful hamlets, pleasant villages, and even tranquil country towns are losing their primitive characters for simplicity and contentment by the passage of these fiery trains, that drag after them a sort of bastard elegance, a pretension that is destructive of peace of mind, and an uneasy desire in all who dwell by the wayside to pry into the mysteries of the whole length and breadth of the region it traverses !

We are writing of the year of our Lord one thousand eight hundred and nineteen. In that day Oyster Pond was, in one of the best acceptations of the word, a rural district. It is true that its inhabitants were accustomed to the water, and to the sight of vessels, from the two-decker to the little shabby-looking craft that brought ashes from town to meliorate the sandy lands of Suffolk Only five years before an English squadron had lain in Gardiner's Bay, here pronounced "Gar'ner's," watching the Race, or eastern outlet of the Sound, with a view to cut off the trade and annoy their enemy. That game is up forever. No hostile squadron, English, French, Dutch, or all united will ever again blockade an American port for any serious length of time—the young Herculese passing too rapidly from the gristle into the bone any longer to suffer antics of this nature to be played in front of his cradle. But such was not his condition in the war of 1812, and the good people of Oyster Pond had become familiar with the checkered sides of two-deck ships, and the venerable and beautiful ensign of Old England, as it floated above them.

Nor was it only by these distant views, and by means of

hostilities, that the good folk of Oyster Pond were acquainted with vessels. New-York is necessary to all on the coast, as a market and as a place to procure supplies; and every creek, or inlet, or basin, of any sort, within a hundred leagues of it, is sure to possess one or more craft that ply between the favorite haven and the particular spot in question. Thus was it with Oyster Pond. There is scarce a better harbor on the whole American coast than that which the narrow arm of the sea that divides the point from Shelter Island presents; and even in the simple times of which we are writing Sterling had its two or three coasters, such as they were. But the true maritime character of Oyster Pond, as well as that of all Suffolk, was derived from the whalers, and its proper nucleus was across the estuary, at Sag-Harbor. Thither the youths of the whole region resorted for employment, and to advance their fortunes, and generally with such success as is apt to attend enterprise, industry, and daring, when exercised with energy in a pursuit of moderate gains. None became rich in the strict signification of the term, though a few got to be in reasonably affluent circumstances; many were placed altogether at their ease, and more were made humbly comfortable. A farm in America is well enough for the foundation of family support, but it rarely suffices for all the growing wants of these days of indulgence, and of a desire to enjoy so much of that which was formerly left to the undisputed possession of the unquestionably rich. A farm, with a few hundreds *per annum* derived from other sources, makes a good base of comfort; and if the hundreds are converted into thousands, your farmer or agriculturist becomes a man not only at his ease, but a proprietor of some importance. The farms on Oyster Pond were 1 either very extensive, nor had they owners of large incomes to support them; on the contrary, most of them were made to support their owners; a thing that is possible, even in America, with industry, frugality, and judgment. In order, however, that the names of places we may have occasion to use shall be understood it may be well to be a little more particular in our preliminary explanation.

The reader knows that we are now writing of Suffolk County, Long Island, New-York. He also knows that our opening scene is to be on the shorter, or most northern, of the two prongs of that fork which divides the eastern end of this island, giving it what are properly two capes. The smallest territorial division that is known to the laws of New-York, in rural districts, is the "township," as it is called. These townships are usually larger than the English parish, corresponding more properly with the French canton. They vary, however, greatly in size, some containing as much as a hundred square miles, which is the largest size, while others do not contain more than a tenth of that surface.

The township in which the northern prong, or point of Long Island, lies, is named Southold, and includes not only all of the long, low, narrow land that then went by the common names of Oyster Pond, Sterling, etc., but several islands also which stretch off in the Sound, as well as a broader piece of territory near Riverhead. Oyster Pond, which is the portion of the township that lies on the "point," is, or *was*—for we write of a remote period in the galloping history of the State—only a part of Southold, and probably was not then a name known in the laws at all.

We have a wish, also, that this name should be pronounced properly. It is not called Oyster *Pond*, as the uninitiated would be very apt to get it, but *Oyster* Pund, the last word having a sound similar to that of the cockney's "pound" in his "two pund two." This discrepancy between the spelling and the pronunciation of proper names is agreeable to us, for it shows that a people are not put in leading strings by pedagogues, and that they make use of their own in their own way. We remember how great was our satisfaction once, on entering Holmes' Hole, a well-known bay in this very vicinity, in our youth, to hear a boatman call the port "Hum'ses Hull." It is getting to be so rare to meet with an American, below the higher classes, who will consent to cast this species of veil before his schoolday acquisitions, that we acknowledge it gives us pleasure to hear such good, homely, old-fashioned English as "Gar'ner's Island," "Hum'ses Hull" and "*Oyster* Pund."

This plainness of speech was not the only proof of the simplicity of former days that was to be found in Suffolk, in the first quarter of the century. The eastern end of Long Island lies so much out of the track of the rest of the world, that even the new railroad cannot make much impression on its inhabitants, who get their pigs and poultry, butter and eggs, a little earlier to market than in the days of the stage-wagons, it is true, but they fortunately, as yet, bring little back except it be the dross that sets everything in motion, whether it be by rail, or through the sands, in the former toilsome mode.

The season, at the precise moment when we desire to take the reader with us to Oyster Pond, was in the delightful month of September, when the earlier promises of the year are fast maturing into performance. Although Suffolk, as a whole, can scarcely be deemed a productive county, being generally of a thin, light soil, and still covered with a growth of small wood, it possesses, nevertheless, spots of exceeding fertility. A considerable portion of the northern prong of the fork has this latter character, and Oyster Pond is a sort of garden compared with much of the sterility that prevails around it. Plain but respectable dwellings, with numerous out-buildings, orchards and fruit-trees, fences carefully preserved, a paintaking tillage, good roads, and here and there a "meeting-house," gave the fork an air of rural and moral beauty that, aided by the water by which it was so nearly surrounded, contributed greatly to relieve the monotony of so dead a level. There were heights in view, on Shelter Island, and bluffs toward Riverhead, which, if they would not attract much attention in Switzerland, were by no means overlooked in Suffolk. In a word, both the season and the place were charming, though most of the flowers had already faded ; and the apple, and the pear, and the peach, were taking the places of the inviting cherry. Fruit abounded, notwithstanding the close vicinity of the district to salt water, the airs from the sea bei; g broken, or somewhat tempered, by the land that lay to the southward.

We have spoken of the coasters that ply between the emporium and all the creeks and bays of the Sound, as well as of the numberless rivers that find an outlet for their waters between Sandy Hook and Rockaway. Wharves were constructed, at favorable points, *inside* the prong, and occasionally a sloop was seen at them loading its truck, or discharging its ashes or street manure ; the latter being a very common return cargo for a Long Island coaster. At one wharf, however, now lay a vessel of a different mould, and one which, though of no great size, was manifestly intended to go *outside*. This was a schooner that had been recently launched, and which had advanced no farther in its first equipment than to get in its two principal spars, the rigging of which hung suspended over the mast-heads, in readiness to be "set up" for the first time. The day being Sunday, work was suspended, and this so much the more, because the owner of the vessel was a certain Deacon Pratt, who dwelt in a house within half a mile of the wharf, and who was also the proprietor of three several parcels of land in that neighborhood, each of which had its own buildings and conveniences, and was properly enough dignified with the name of a farm. To be sure, neither of these farms was very large, their acres united amounting to but little more than two hundred ; but, owing to their condition the native richness of the soil, and the mode of turning them to account, they had made Deacon Pratt a warm man for Suffolk.

There are two great species of deacons ; for we suppose they must all be referred to the same *genera*. One species belong to the priesthood, and become priests and bishops ; passing away, as priests and bishops are apt to do, with more or less of the savor of godliness. The other species are purely laymen, and are *sui generis*. They are, *ex officio*, the most pious men in the neighborhood, as they sometimes are, as it would seem to us, *ex-officio*, also the most grasping and mercinary. As we are not in the secrets of the sects to which these lay-deacons belong, we shall not presume to pronounce whether the individual is elevated to the deaconate because he is prosperous, in a worldly sense, or whether the prosperity is a consequence of the deaconate; but, that the two usually go together is quite certain; which being the cause, and which the effect, we leave to wiser heads to determine.

Deacon Pratt was no exception to the rule. A tighter-fisted sinner did not exist in the county than this pious soul, who certainly not only wore, but wore out the "form of godliness," while he was devoted, heart and hand. to the daily increase of worldly gear. No one spoke disparagingly of the deacon, notwithstanding. So completely had he got to be interwoven with the church—"meeting," we ought to say—in that vicinity, that speaking disparagingly of him would have appeared like assailing Christianity. It is true, that many an unfortunate fellow citizen in Suffolk had been made to feel how close was the gripe of his hand, when he found himself in its grasp; but there is a way of practising the most ruthless extortion, that serves not only to deceive the world, but which would really seem to mislead the extortioner himself. Phrases take the place of deeds, sentiments those of facts, and grimaces those of benevolent looks, so ingeniously and so impudently that the wronged often fancy that they are the victims of a severe dispensation of Providence, when the truth would have shown that they were simply robbed.

We do not mean, however, that Deacon Pratt was a robber. He was merely a hard man in the management of his affairs, never cheating, in a direct sense, but seldom conceding a cent to generous impulses, or to the duties of kind. He was a widower, and childless, circumstances that rendered his love of gain still less pardonable; for many man who is indifferent to money on his own account, will toil and save to lay up hords for those who are to come after him The deacon had only a niece to inherit his effects, unless he might choose to step beyond that degree of consanguinity, and bestow a portion of his means on cousins. The church—or, to be more literal, the "meeting"—had an eye to his resources, however; and it was whispered it had actually succeeded. by means known to itself, in squeezing out of his tight grasp no less a sum than one hundred dollars, as a donation to a certain theological college. It was conjectured by some persons that this was only the beginning of a religious liberality, and that the excellent and goodly-minded deacon would bestow most of his property in a similar way, when the moment should come that it could be no longer of any use to himself. This opinion was much in favor with divers devout females of the deacon's congregation, who had daughters of their own, and who seldom failed to conclude their observations on this interesting subject with some such remark as, "Well, in *that* case, and it seems to me that everything points that way, Mary Pratt will get no more than any other poor man's daughter."

Little did Mary, the only child of Israel Pratt, an elder brother of the deacon, think of all this. She had been left an orphan in her tenth year, both parents dying within a few months of each other, and had lived beneath her uncle's roof for nearly ten more years, until use, and natural affection, and the customs of the country, had made her feel absolutely at home there. A less interested, or less selfish being than Mary Pratt, never existed. In this respect she was the very antipodes of her uncle, who often stealthily rebuked her for her charities and acts of neighborly kindness, which he was wont to term waste. But Mary kept the even tenor of her way, seemingly not hearing such remarks, and doing her duty quietly, and in all humility.

Suffolk was settled originally by emigrants from New England, and the character of its people is to this hour of modified New England habits and notions. Now one of the marked peculiarities of Connecticut is an indisposition to part with anything without a *quid pro quo*. Those little services, offerings and conveniencies that are elsewhere parted with without a thought of remuneration, go regularly upon the day-book, and often reappear on a "settlement," years after they have been forgotten by those who received the favors. Even the man who keeps a carriage will let it out for hire; and the manner in which money is accepted,

and even asked for by persons in easy circumstances, and
for things that would be gratuitous in the Middle States,
often causes disappointment, and sometimes disgust. In
this particular Scottish and Swiss thrift, both notorious,
and the latter particularly so, are nearly equalled by New
England thrift; more especially in the close estimate of
the value of services rendered. So marked, indeed, is this
practice of looking for requitals, that even the language is
infected with it. Thus, should a person pass a few months
by invitation with a friend, his visit is termed "boarding;"
it being regarded as a matter of course that he pays his
way. It would scarcely be safe, indeed, without the precaution of "passing receipts" on quitting, for one to stay
any time in a New England dwelling, unless prepared to
pay for his board. The free and frank habits that prevail
among relatives and friends elsewhere, are nearly unknown
there, every service having its price. These customs are
exceedingly repugnant to all who have been educated in
different notions; yet they are not without their redeeming
qualities, that might be pointed out to advantage, though
our limits will not permit us, at this moment so to do.

Little did Mary Pratt suspect the truth; but habit, or
covetousness, or some vague expectation that the girl might
yet contract a marriage that would enable him to claim all
his advances, had induced the deacon never to bestow a
cent on her education, or dress, or pleasures of any sort,
that the money was not regularly charged against her in
that nefarious work he called his "day-book." As for the
self-respect, and the feelings of cast, which prevent a gentleman from practising any of these tradesmen's tricks, the
deacon knew nothing of them. He would have set the
man down as a fool who deferred to any notions so unprof-
itable. With him not only every *man*, but every *thing*,
"had its price," and usually it was a good price too. At
the very moment when our tale opens, there stood charged
in his book, against his unsuspecting and affectionate niece
items in the way of schooling, dress, board, and pocket
money, that amounted to the considerable sum of one
thousand dollars, money fairly expended. The deacon was

only intensely mean and avaricious, while he was as honest as the day. Not a cent was overcharged ; and, to own the truth, Mary was so great a favorite with him that most of his charges against *her* were rather of a reasonable rate than otherwise.

On the Sunday in question, Deacon Pratt went to meeting as usual, the building in which divine service was held that day, standing less than two miles from his residence : but, instead of remaining for the afternoon's preaching, as was his wont, he got into his one-horse chaise, the vehicle then in universal use among the middle classes, though now so seldom seen, and skirred away homeward as fast as an active, well-fed, and powerful switch-tailed mare could draw him ; the animal being accompanied in her rapid progress by a colt of some three months existence. The residence of the deacon was unusually inviting for a man of his narrow habits. It stood on the edge of a fine apple-orchard, having a door-yard of nearly two acres in its front. This door-yard, which had been twice mown that summer, was prettily embellished with flowers, and was shaded by four rows of noble cherry-trees. The house itself was of wood, as is almost uniformly the case in Suffolk, where little stone is to be found, and where brick constructions are apt to be thought damp ; but it was a respectable edifice, with five windows in front, and of two stories. The siding was of unpainted cedar shingles ; and, although the house had been erected long previously to the Revolution, the siding had been renewed but once, about ten years before the opening of our tale, and the whole building was in a perfect state of repair. The thrift of the deacon rendered him careful, and he was thoroughly convinced of the truth of the familiar adage which tells us that "a stitch in time saves nine." All around the house and farm was in perfect order, proving the application of the saying. As for the view, it was sufficiently pleasant, the house having its front toward the east, while its end windows looked, the one set in the direction of the Sound, and the other in that of the arm of the sea, which belongs properly to Peconic Bay, we believe. All this water, some of which was visible over points and among islands, together with a smiling and fertile, though narrow stretch of fore-ground, could not fail of making an agreeable landscape.

It was little, however, that Deacon Pratt thought of views, or beauty of any sort, as the mare reached the open gate of his own abode. Mary was standing in the stoop, or porch of the house, and appeared to be anxiously awaiting her uncle's return. The latter gave the reins to a black, one who was no longer a slave, but who was a descendant of some of the ancient slaves of the Pratts, and in that character consented still to dawdle about the place, working for half price. On alighting, the uncle approached the niece with somewhat of interest in his manner.

"Well, Mary," said the former, "how does he get on now?"

"Oh! my dear sir, he cannot possibly live, I think, and I do most earnestly entreat that you will let me send across to the Harbor for Dr. Sage."

By the Harbor was meant Sag's, and the physician named was one of merited celebrity in old Suffolk. So healthy was the country in general, and so simple were the habits of the people, that neither lawyer nor physician was to be found in every hamlet, as is the case to-day. Both were to be had at Riverhead, as well as at Sag-Harbor; but, if a man called out "Squire," or "Doctor," in the highways of Suffolk, sixteen men did not turn round to reply, as is said to be the case in other regions; one half answering to the one appellation, and the second half to the other. The deacon had two objections to yielding to his niece's earnest request; the expense being one, though it was not in this instance the greatest; there was another reason that he kept to himself, but which will appear as our narrative proceeds.

A few weeks previously to the Sunday in question, a sea going vessel, inward bound, had brought up in Gardiner's Bay, which is a usual anchorage for all sorts of craft. A worn-out and battered seaman had been put ashore on Oyster Pond, by a boat from this vessel, which sailed to the westward soon after, proceeding most probably to New

York. The stranger was not only well advanced in life, but he was obviously wasting away with disease.

The account given of himself by this seaman was sufficiently explicit. He was born on Martha's Vinyard, but, as is customary with the boys of that island, he had left home in his twelfth year, and had now been absent from the place of his birth a little more than half a century. Conscious of the decay which beset him, and fully convinced that his days were few and numbered, the seaman who called himself Tom Daggett, had felt a desire to close his eyes in the place where they had first been opened to the light of day. He had persuaded the commander of the craft mentioned to bring him from the West Indies, and to put him ashore as related, the Vineyard being only a hundred miles or so to the eastward of Oyster Pond Point. He trusted to luck to give him the necessary opportunity of overcoming these last hundred miles.

Daggett was poor, as he admitted, as well as friendless and unknown. He had with him, nevertheless, a substantial sea-chest, one of those that the sailors of that day uniformly used in merchant-vessels, a man-of-war compelling them to carry their clothes in bags, for the convenience of compact stowage. The chest of Daggett, however, was a regular inmate of the forecastle, and, from its appearance, had made almost as many voyages as its owner. The last indeed, was heard to say that he had succeeded in saving it from no less than three shipwrecks. It was a reasonably heavy chest, though its contents, when opened, did not seem to be of any great value.

A few hours after landing this man had made a bargain with a middle-aged widow, in very humble circumstances, and who dwelt quite near to the residence of Deacon Pratt, to receive him as a temporary inmate ; or, until he could get a "chance across to the Vineyard." At first Daggett kept about, and was much in the open air. While able to walk he met the deacon, and singular—nay, unaccountable as it seemed to the niece—the uncle soon contracted a species of friendship for, not to say intimacy with, this stranger. In the first place, the deacon was a little particular in not

having intimates among the necessitous, and the Widow
White soon let it be known that her guest had not even a
"red cent." He had chattels, however, that were of some
estimation among seamen; and Roswell Gardiner, or "Gar-
'ner," as he was called, the young seaman *par excellence* of
the Point, one who had been not only a-whaling, but who
had also been a-sealing, and who at that moment was on
board the deacon's schooner, in the capacity of master, had
been applied to for advice and assistance. By the agency
of Mr. Gar'ner, as the young mate was then termed, sundry
palms, sets of sail-needles, a fid or two, and various similar
articles, that obviously could no longer be of any use to
Daggett, were sent across to the "Harbor," and disposed of
there, to advantage, among the many seamen of that port.
By these means the stranger was, for a few weeks, enabled
to pay his way, the board he got being both poor and
cheap.

A much better result attended this intercourse with Gardiner than that of raising the worn-out seaman's immediate
ways and means. Between Mary Pratt and Roswell Gardiner there existed an intimacy of long standing for their
years, as well as of some peculiar features, to which there
will be occasion to advert hereafter. Mary was the very
soul of charity in all its significations, and this Gardiner
knew. When, therefore, Daggett became really necessitous
in the way of comforts that even money could not command
beneath the roof of Widow White, the young man let the
fact be known to the deacon's niece, who immediately pro-
vided sundry delicacies that were acceptable to the palate
of even disease. As for her uncle, nothing was at first
said to him on the subject. Although his intimacy with
Daggett went on increasing, and they were daily more and
more together in long and secret conference, not a suggestion was ever made by the deacon in the way of contribut-
ing to his new friend's comforts. To own the truth, to give
was the last idea that ever occurred to this man's thoughts.

Mary Pratt was observant, and of a mind so constituted
that its observations usually led her to safe and accurate
deductions. Great was the surprise of all on the Point

when it became known that Deacon Pratt had purchased and put into the water the new sea-going craft that was building on speculation at Southold. Not only had he done this, but he had actually bought some half-worn copper, and had it placed on the schooner's bottom, as high as the bends, ere he had her launched. While the whole neighborhood was "exercised" with conjectures on the motive which could induce the deacon to become a ship-owner in his age, Mary did not fail to impute it to some secret but powerful influence that the sick stranger had obtained over him. He now spent nearly half his time in private communications with Daggett; and, on more than one occasion, when the niece had taken some light article of food over for the use of the last, she found him and her uncle examining one or two dirty and well-worn charts of the ocean. Not only was the schooner purchased, and coppered and launched, and preparations made to fit her for sea, but "young Gar'ner" was appointed to command her.

Here follows an account of Roswell Gardiner and his ancestry, and more about him and Mary Pratt, which is omitted.

Such was the state of things when the deacon returned from meeting, as related in the opening chapter. At his niece's suggestion of sending to the Harbor for Dr. Sage, he had demurred, not only on account of the expense, but for a still more cogent reason. To tell the truth, he was exceedingly distrustful of any one's being admitted to a communication with Daggett, who had revealed to him matters that he deemed to be of great importance, but who still retained the key to his most material mystery. Nevertheless, decency, to say nothing of the influence of what folks "would say," the Archimedean lever of all society of puritanical origin, exhorted him to consent to his niece's proposal.

"It is such a roundabout road to get to the Harbor, Mary," the uncle slowly objected, after a pause.

"Boats often go there, and return in a few hours."

"Yes, yes—*boats ;* but I'm not certain it is lawful to work boats of a Sabbath, chill."

"I believe, sir, it was deemed lawful to do good on the Lord's day."

"Yes, if a body was certain it *would* do any good. To be sure, Sage is a capital doctor—as good as any going in these parts—but, half the time, money paid for doctor's stuff is thrown away.

"Still, I think it our duty to try to serve a fellow-creature that is in distress ; and Daggett, I fear, will not go through the week, if indeed he go through the night."

"I should be sorry to have him die !" exclaimed the deacon, looking really distressed at this intelligence. "Right sorry should I be to have him die—just yet."

The last two words were uttered unconsciously, and in a way to cause the niece to regret that they had been uttered at all. But they had come, notwithstanding, and the deacon saw that he had been too frank. The fault could not now be remedied, and he was fain to allow his words to produce their own effect.

"Die he will, I fear, uncle," returned Mary, after a short pause ; "and sorry should I be to have it so without our feeling the consolation of knowing we had done all in our power to save him, or to serve him."

"It is so far to the Harbor, that no good might come of a messenger; and the money paid *him* would be thrown away, too."

"I dare say Roswell Gar'ner would be glad to go to help a fellow-creature who is suffering. *He* would not think of demanding any pay."

"Yes, that is true. I will say this for Gar'ner, that he is as reasonable a young man, when he does an odd job, as any one I know. I like to employ him."

Mary understood this very well. It amounted to neither more nor less than the deacon's perfect conscientiousness that the youth had, again and again, given him his time and his services gratuitously ; and that, too, more than once, under circumstances when it would have been quite proper that he should look for a remuneration. A slight color stole over the face of the niece as memory recalled to her mind these different occasions. Was that sensitive blush owing to her perceiving the besetting weakness of one who stood in the light of a parent to her, and toward whom she endeavored to feel the affection of a child? We shall not gainsay this, so far as a portion of the feeling which produced that blush was concerned; but, certain it is, that the thought that Roswell had exerted himself to oblige *her* uncle, obtruded itself somewhat vividly among her other recollections.

"Well, sir," the niece resumed, after another brief pause, "we can send for Roswell, if you think it best, and ask him to do the poor man this act of kindness."

"Your messengers after doctors are always in such a hurry! I dare say Gar'ner would think it necessary to hire a horse to cross Shelter Island, and then perhaps a boat to get across to the Harbor. If no boat was to be found, it might be another horse to gallop away round the head of the Bay. Why, five dollars would scarce meet the cost of such a race!"

"If five dollars were needed, Roswell would pay them out of his own pocket, rather than ask another to assist him in doing an act of charity. But, no horse will be necessary; the whale-boat is at the wharf, and is ready for use at any moment."

"True, I had forgotten the whale-boat. If that is home the doctor might be brought across at a reasonable rate, especially if Gar'ner will volunteer. I dare say Daggett's effects will pay the bill for attendance, since they have answered, as yet, to meet the Widow White's charges. As I live, here comes Gar'ner at this moment, and just as we want him."

"I knew of no other to ask to cross the bays, sir, and sent for Roswell before you returned. Had you not got back as you did, I should have taken on myself the duty of sending for the doctor."

"In which case, girl, you would have made yourself liable. I have too many demands on my means to be scattering dollars broadcast. But, here is Gar'ner, and I dare say all will be made right."

Gardiner now joined the uncle and niece, who had held

this conversation in the porch, having hastened up from the schooner the instant he received Mary's summons. He was rewarded by a kind look and a friendly shake of the hand, each of which was slightly more cordial than those that prudent and thoughtful young woman was accustomed to bestow on him. He saw that Mary was a little earnest in her manner, and looked curious, as well as interested, to learn why he had been summoned at all. Sunday was kept so rigidly at the deacon's that the young man did not dare visit the house until after the sun had set; the New England practice of commencing the Sabbath of a Saturday evening, and bringing it to a close at the succeeding sunset, prevailing among most of the people of Suffolk, the Episcopalians forming nearly all the exceptions to the usage. Sunday evening, consequently, was in great request for visits, it being the favorite time for the young people to meet, as they were not only certain to be unemployed, but to be in their best. Roswell Gardiner was in the practice of visiting Mary Pratt Sunday evenings; but he would almost as soon think of desecrating a church, as think of entering the deacon's abode, on the Sabbath, until after sunset, or "sundown," to use the familiar Americanism that is commonly applied to this hour of the day. Here he was now, however, wondering, and anxious to learn why he had been sent for.

"Roswell," said Mary earnestly, slightly coloring again as she spoke, "we have a great favor to ask. You know the poor old sailor who has been staying at the Widow White's this month or more—he is now very low; so low, we think he ought to have better advice than can be found on Oyster Pond, and we wish to get Dr. Sage over from the Harbor. How to do it has been the question, when I thought of you. If you could take the whale-boat and go across, the poor man might have the benefit of the doctor's advice in the course of a few hours."

"Yes," put in the uncle, "and I shall charge nothing for the use of the boat; so that, if *you* volunteer, Gar'ner, it will leave so much towards settling up the man's accounts when settling-day comes."

Roswell Gardiner understood both uncle and niece perfectly. The intense selfishness of the first was no more a
secret to him than was the entire disinterestedness of the
last. He gazed a moment, in fervent admiration, at Mary;
then he turned to the deacon, and professed his readiness
to "volunteer." Knowing the man so well, he took care
distinctly to express the word, so as to put the mind of
this votary of Mammon at ease.

"Gar'ner will *volunteer*, then," rejoined the uncle, "and I
shall charge nothing for the use of the boat. This is 'doing as we would be done by,' and is all right, considering
that Daggett is sick and among strangers. The wind is
fair, or nearly fair, to go and to come back, and you'll make
a short trip of it. Yes, it will cost nothing, and may do
the poor man good."

"Now go at once, Roswell," said Mary, in an entreating
manner; "and show the same skill in managing the boat
that you did the day you won the race against the Harbor
oarsmen"

"I will do all that a man can, to oblige you, Mary, as
well as to serve the sick. If Dr. Sage should not be at
home, am I to look for another physician, Mr. Pratt?"

"Sage *must* be at home—we can employ no other. Your
old, long-established physicians understand how to consider
practice, and don't make mistakes—by the way, Gar'ner,
you needn' mention *my* name in the business at all. Just
say that a sick man, at the Widow White's, needs his services, and that you had *volunteered* to take him across.
That will bring him—I know the man."

Again Gardiner understood what the deacon meant. He
was just as desirous of not paying the physician as of not
paying the messenger. Mary understood him, too, and
with a face more sad than anxiety had previously made it
she walked into the house, leaving her uncle and lover in
the porch. After a few more injunctions from the former,
in the way of prudent precaution, the latter departed, hur-
rying down to the water-side in order to take the boat.

The narrative than discloses that the interest which
Deacon Pratt had in Daggett, and his many interviews

with him, was owing to the fact that the sick seaman had disclosed to him that he had two important secrets. One was that he had a knowledge of the exact spot in the South Seas where pirates had buried a considerable amount of treasure, and another, that he knew of certain previously unvisited islands, in low southern latitudes, where seals existed in great abundance. When, in consequence of his feeble condition, he had to be put ashore on Oyster Pond Point, he was on his way to Martha's Vinyard, where he belonged, to make an arrangement for the fitting out of a vessel to go to these two important places, and as such a vessel was as easily obtained in Sag-Harbor, it was for the purpose of making this voyage that Deacon Pratt had purchased the Sea Lion, which he was then fitting up, and of which Foswell Gardiner was to go out as master.

No effort, however, or ingenuity on the part of the Deacon, could procure from the mariner the latitude and longitude of these two places, in the hope that he might recover and go out in the vessel himself, and give this important information to the master when it became necessary. The narrative continues as follows :

Dr. Sage now arrived ; a shrewd. observant, intelligent man, who had formerly represented the district in which he lived in Congress. He was skilful in his profession, and soon made up his mind concerning the state of his patient. As the deacon never left him for a moment, to him he first communicated his opinion, after the visit, as the two walked back toward the well-known dwelling of the Pratts.

"This poor man is in the last stages of a decline," said the physician, coolly, "and medicine can do him no good. He *may* live a month ; though it would not surprise me to hear of his death in an hour."

"Do you think his time so short !" exclaimed the deacon ; "I was in hopes he might last until the Sea Lion goes out, and that a voyage might help to set him up."

"Nothing will ever set him up again, deacon, you may depend on that. No sea-voyage will do him any good; and it is better that he should remain on shore, on account of the greater comforts he will get. Does he belong on Oyster Pond?"

"He comes from somewhere east," answered the deacon, careful not to let the doctor know the place whence the stranger had come, though to little purpose, as will presently be seen. "He has neither friend nor acquaintance here; though I should think his effects sufficient to meet all charges."

"Should they not be, he is welcome to my visit," answered the doctor, promptly; for he well understood the deacon's motive in making the remark. "I have enjoyed a pleasant sail across the bays with young Gar'ner, who has promised to take me back again. I like boating, and am always better for one of these sailing excursions. Could I carry my patients along, half of them would be benefitted by the pure air and the exercise."

"It's a grateful thing to meet with one of your temperament, doctor; but Daggett—"

"Is this man named Daggett?" interrupted the physician.

"I *believe* that is what he calls himself, though a body never is certain of what such people say."

"That's true, deacon; your rambling, houseless sailor is commonly a great liar—at least, so have I always found him. Most of their log books will not do to read; or, for that matter, to be written out in full. But if this man's name is really Daggett, he must come from the Vineyard. There are Daggetts there in scores; yes, he must be a Vineyard man."

"There are Daggetts in Connecticut, as I know, of a certainty—"

"We all know that, for it is a name of weight there; but the Vineyard is the cradle of the breed. The man has a Vineyard look about him, too. I dare say, now, he has not been home for many a day."

The deacon was in an agony. He was menaced with the

very thing he was in the hope of staving off, or a discussion on the subject of the sick man's previous life. The doctor was so mercurial and quick of apprehension, that, once fairly on the scent, he was nearly certain he would extract everything from the patient. This was the principal reason why the deacon did not wish to send for him ; the expense though a serious objection to one so niggardly, being of secondary consideration when so many doubloons were at stake. It was necessary, however, to talk on boldly, as any appearance of hesitation might excite the doctor's distrust. The answers, therefore, came instantaneously.

"It may be as you say, doctor," returned the deacon ; "for them Vineyard folks (Anglice folk) are great wanderers."

"That they are. I had occasion to pass a day there, a few years since, on my way to Boston, and I found five women on the island to one man. It must be a particularly conscientious person who could pass a week there, and escape committing the crime of bigamy. As for your bachelors, I have heard that a poor wretch of that description, who unluckily found himself cast ashore there, was married three times the same morning."

As the doctor was a little of a wag, Deacon Pratt did not deem it necessary religiously to believe all that now escaped him ; but he was glad to keep him in this vein, in order to prevent his getting again on the track of Daggett's early life. The device succeeded, Martha's Vineyard being a standing joke for all in that quarter of the world, on the subject of the ladies.

Mary was in the porch to receive her uncle and the physician. It was unnecessary for her to ask any questions, for her speaking countenance said all that was required in order to obtain an answer.

"He's in a bad way, certainly, young lady," observed the doctor, taking a seat on one of the benches, "and I can give no hope. How long he may live is another matter. If he has friends whom he wishes to see, or if he has any affairs to settle, the truth should be told him at once, and no time lost."

"He knows nothing of his friends," interrupted the deacon, quite thrown off his guard by his own eagerness, and unconscious, at the moment, of the manner in which he was committing himself on the subject of a knowledge of the sick man's birth-place, "not having been on the Vineyard, or heard from there, since he first left home, quite fifty years since."

The doctor saw the contradiction, and it set him thinking, and conjecturing, but he was too discreet to betray himself. An explanation there probably was, and he trusted to time to ascertain it.

"What has become of Captain Gar'ner?" he asked, looking curiously around, as if he expected to find him tied to the niece's apron-string.

Mary blushed, but she was too innocent to betray any real confusion.

"He has gone back to the schooner, in order to have the boat ready for your return."

"And that return must take place, young lady, as soon as I have drunk two cups of your tea. I have patients at the Harbor who must yet be visited this evening, and the wind goes down with the sun. Let the poor man take the draughts I have left for him—they will soothe him, and help his breathing—more than this my skill can do nothing for him. Deacon, you need say nothing of my visit—I am sufficiently repaid by the air, the sail, and Miss Mary's welcome. I perceive that she is glad to see me, and that is something, between so young a woman and so old a man. And now for the two cups of tea."

The tea was drunk, and the doctor took his leave, shaking his head as he repeated to the niece, that the medical science could do nothing for the sick man.

That night Daggett dies without revealing the latitude and longitude of the places. The Sea Lion goes on the voyage to find them with the aid of an old chart found in the seaman's sea-chest, and a series of adventures follow.

D.

LETTERS,

——:o:——

The following letters and extracts from letters, written by Dr. Ebenezer Sage, in the early part of this century, have been selected from letters of the doctor in possession of ex-Chief Justice Charles P. Daly, being regarded as of sufficient interest to be published:

AN ACCOUNT OF DR. EDENEZER SAGE, BY WM. S. PELLETREAU, IN A NOTE TO THE RECORDS OF SOUTHAMPTON, VOL. III, PAGE 363.

Dr. Ebenezer Sage was for many years a prominent citizen of Sag-Harbor. He was born in Portland, Ct., 1755. He studied the profession of medicine and came to East-Hampton, N. Y., in 1789, where he practiced 13 years. He married Ruth, daughter of Dr. Wm. Smith, of Southampton, in 1790, and went to his native place and remained five years, and from thence removed to Sag-Harbor in 1801. He was elected to Congress in 1809 and served three terms. He was a member of the Convention that formed the State Constitution in 1821, and also held the office of Master in Chancery. He died January 20th, 1834, and his wife Ruth died in May, 1831, aged 66. Their remains, after resting many years in the old burying ground at Sag-Harbor, were removed to Oakland Cemetery, Sag-Harbor.

He was a man of elevated character and utterly above the craft and chicanary which too often characterized politicians Although he had the faculty of expressing his thoughts in writing with much facility, he had not the command of words which makes the orator, and in his congressional career, and as a member of the Constitutional Convention, he was never absent from his seat and never failed to vote on every question, and never made a speech.

He was a descendant of David Sage, who came to this country from Wales about 1660, and died in 1704, and is buried in the old cemetery at Middletown, Ct. David Sage left two sons, John and Timothy; the latter had a son David who was the father of the subject of the above sketch. Dr. Ebenezer had one son, Dr. John Sage, for many years a physician in Sag-Harbor, and lived in the old gamble roofed house east of the Episcopal Church, north side of Sage street, which was named in his honor.

ON PUBLIC AFFAIRS IN CONNECTICUT.

CHATHAM, Sept. 13, 1800.

DEAR FRIEND:

Notwithstanding you are two or three letters in my debt, yet as Topping is here I will risque another small item to the account, and just remind you that if the whole is not soon balanced I shall begin to calculate interest.

The next day after to-morrow will be the great, the important day when the freemen of the state will assemble to choose what they call Deputies to the General Assembly. The state was never before in such agitation, the British federalists fear the republicans will be able to elect a majority of their own sentiments into the State Legislature, which will give Mr. Jefferson 9 Electors, or none for either of the Candidates—they likewise fear 2 or 3 republican characters will find their way into the next Congress, &c. This has roused the ire of half the little petty foggers in the state. Our federal Newspapers have for some weeks teemed with the grossest scurrillity and abuse of Mr. Jefferson. That capacious squirt, of political filth, *The Courant* has for some time past been discharging the most abominable torrents of calumny and blackgardism that ever issued from any press in the country, they even suggest that should Mr. Jefferson be elected he would blow down all the Meetinghouses and hang all the priests, and to this our Pulpits resound with the most dreadful Anathemas against those who support such a vile Atheist, and they prove him an Atheist to demonstration, from the amount he has given us he in his Notes on Virginia of the Bones, the Oyster Shells, and the Indians—so it goes. I doubt the issue, the old cry, "the Church is in danger" will dupe a great many well meaning men.

Yours truly,

E. SAGE.

To HENRY P. DERING, SAG-HARBOR, N. Y., DESCRIBING THE INCONVENIENCIES OF TRAVELING AT THAT DATE.

WASHINGTON, Dec. 6th, 1810.

MY DEAR FRIEND:

I arrived at this place on the 4th, a week from New-York; through perils by flood and field: foundered in the mud at midnight in New Jersey and obliged to hire the driver to watch the baggage 'till morning and then send him after a Jersey farmer to come with his ox team and drag the stage out of the mire. The next night befogged and becalmed upon the Deleware, and then caught in a violent tempest of wind and snow and hail upon the Chesapeak, so dark that our Captain cast anker for fear that he should run upon Pools Island; his anker dragged and he was obliged to put over his best bower and ride out the storm until morning, when we found oveselves so near the Island and the tempest so violent that our Captain was obliged to slip his cable, and in a short time we were in Baltimore at the rate of 12 nots an hour; from Baltimore (40 miles) the stages were in many places near hub deep in snow and mud.

On the Chesapeake I passed a very uncomfortable night. There was 80 passengers and but 18 berths, we drew for them and I unfortunately drew a blank, of course was compelled to sleep in my chair or not sleep at all. I should have left New-York a day or two earlier, but Dr. Mitchel persuaded me to take the steamboat line with him, but I lost him at Brunswick and never saw anything more of him until I arrived at the city. My stage companions most of the way from Brunswick were 7 federalists, among whom was Laban Wheaton and notwithstanding our perils and disappointments I never had a more diverting journey.

The two days I have been here have spent in hearing documents, they are very voluminous, I will send them on as soon as they are printed. I have nothing of news to tell you and cannot at present say what will be the completion of the session, tempestious or calm. I believe however it will be the less stormy than the last, our course of duty is plain, if we have wisdom and firmness to pursue it. Of all this I can judge better when the battle begins.

Sawyer has not yet made his appearance. They are telling a good story about him here. That not long since he agreed to marry a young lady, and they appointed a day; on which day he was observed to be making preparations for a journey; a friend asked him if he had not forgotten that he must be married on that day; he started and said it had really slipped his memory, but that he would fulfill his promise, which he accordingly did and set off upon his journey the next day, and has not been heard of since.

I am anxious how my family will fare, especially if John goes to New York. Will you be good enough, occasionally to call in and know their wants? John, when I left him in New York, agreed to return and spend two or three months in the office of Miller and Gardiner and I engaged board for him at Eldredges, as I hope that he will not relinquish the plan. He appeared to be much pleased with New York especially the Play and steam engine. I took him with me to visit Dr. Jn. C. Osborn who gave him an invitation to visit his house and become acquainted with his young Gent'n and attend Chemecal Lectures, &c.

Remember me to Mrs. Dering and the family.

Yours truly,

E. SAGE.

ADDRESSED TO HENRY P. DERING, SAG-HARBOR, N. Y.

WASHINGTON, May 10th, 1812.

DEAR FRIEND:

It is Sunday and G—— has exchanged for me a $20 Manhattan Note for one on the Washington bank. It was all he had of that description and considering your distress I have thought it best to send it on, notwithstanding it compels me to write another letter, and what to write I know not; not that there is any want of matter. If we take up politics, both as it respects the general government or our own, and still less if we grope through the dirty, blind allies of intrigue, and political swingling—but this is a disgusting subject, and particularly here, the great resevoir, into which are emptied all the dirty rills of filth from all quarters of the union, but more from the state of the Manhattoes than all the others. For three or four years past politics is all together a matter of bargain and sale, with them like their merchantile speculations. Give me offices and I will give you votes, help out our bank, or set types for us and we will give you stock, money and jobs, scratch my back and I will scratch your elbow.

I have learned the secret about our friend S——'s late management. I am not at liberty to tell you the particulars. It is of a nature however to move my sorrow rather than excite any other passion. Necessity has no laws you know. Poor fellow I pity him, he would be honest if he dare—a man who is strugling for existance his and that of his family will often kiss the rod of power, that he would despise with a noble daring in other circumstances—

Enough of this, let me fill up the paper with lighter matter. I was last Wednesday evening at Dolly's Levee, where Coles, the President's secretary informed me that the President wishes me to take a family dinner with him on Saturday at 3 o'clock—a select mess of 6 or 7. This promises something besides eating and drinking which his public dinners do not; consisting generally of about 30. I was there at the hour and we were entertained until 4 with desultory conversation and looking at the pretty things the good Lady presented us, such as needle work, drawings and dead birds embalmed with tow or some other kind of stuffing, which the Ladies of Philadelphia and elsewhere had sent her, and dedicated to her as the Protectres of the fine arts. At 4 we sat down to dinner, Gen. Brown and Smiley from Pennsylvania, old Gov'n Penier of Tenn., Morrow from Ohio, Green from Massachusetts and Albert Gallitin formerly of Geneva now of Washington and myself, 7, besides the President and Dolly and Mr. Secretary, not of foreign but of home relations. After finishing our Beef and other meats and fish, the desert and wine was brought on, consisting of various kinds of eatables such as Icecream, Walnuts, Chestnuts, peanuts, Jellies and sweetmeats, fruit and various species of cake the names of which I am ignorant. Over this light stuff we sat until sunset, talking of almost everything but politics, when we took french leave and departed to our homes all perfectly sober.

I know not when I have laughed more in a given time—a few glasses of Wine soon broke down all distinction betwixt us small folks and the master of the feast, brought something like a maiden blush upon the little man's cheek and elevated him just high enough for anecdotes, of which he has an inexhaustable fund, relates them admirable well, with a chaste and pure style and considerable comic humor, not a word too much or too little, he will relate 30 in the same time some men would one. Here acted in a character I never before saw him, that of a social companion. In general he is sedate and as modest as a nun. It was a family dinner and the only one I ever enjoyed at his house. Our dinner parties here are generally so numerous that I should prefer staying at home and dining upon salt herring. When I look upon this little man and see him struggling with the honest and most persevering industry of a good patriot, to stem the torrent of abuse and corruption that is setting in upon him, foreign and domestic, I pity him, that his lot has fallen on such evil times.

He has not been ten rods from his house this winter, except at the burial of the Vice President, and then he came near having his neck broken by the fright of his horses at the firing of the marines into the grave of the old Gentleman. He appears to be in good health, but as light as a gull. What there is of him must be of brass, if he can live 3 years longer, in the times that are approaching, assailed by scoundrels of all degrees and metres, some endeavoring to kick him out of the way, and others to get jobs out of him. Napolion's situation is not so laborious and difficult, he has nobody's will to consult or pursue but his own and has half a million of bayonets to carry it into execution.

Good Morning,

E. SAGE.

ADDRESSED: DOCTOR WILLIAM CRAWFORD, GETTYSBURG, ADAMS COUNTY, PENNSYLVANIA.

SAG-HARBOR, July 24th, 1814.

DEAR FRIEND:

You must pay a pistareen to the Revenue for this letter which is in greater need of the money than you are, I therefore tax you that sum *pro bono publico*, and as it respects yourself I shall endeavor to give you the worth of the money in news. Should we in this quarter make daily or weekly reports of the movements of the British squadron, their acts and doings, we could furnish as rich a report for the *quid nuncs*, as the reporters on the Chesapeake. Our blockading squadron is often as large as theirs and quite as mischevious. On my return here last spring, 7 of their floating bastions were at the mouth of this harbor taking in water from a little island which they have in possession and where they fat their Yankee cattle which come to them too lean for immediate use. Yesterday the squadron consisted of 5 ships, to-day only two, their boats are every night out in all directions in pursuit of coasters, trade and plunder. Yesterday two deserters were here from the Superb. They took a boat from one of the ship's tenders and landed about 20 miles from this and travelled nearly all the distance without entering a house, being told on board the ship that the American government had agreed to send all deserters back to be hanged. One of them, a frenchman by birth but brought up in Ireland, the other a prussian, both young and intelligent and say they were impressed. They report that on board the fleet the talk is, that they expect every day a fleet of 16 men-of-war and Wellington's army to come into the Sound, land upon Long Island and take New York, and that the Sylph (a sloop of war) which has been on this station all summer sailed about 6 days ago to look up and pilot in this huge fleet. It is a fact that the Sylph has been missing many days. The people furnished these poor tars with some money and they have started for New York, where we learn a great alarm prevails in consequence of intelligence from various quarters that their city is the object of the banditti lately arrived at Halifax. The whole country is in motion throwing up works at Hellgate, Brooklin heights, &c.

You will recollect a Joshua Penny who was last summer taken from his bed near this by the crew of a British barge carried on board the Ramillies, put in irons and upon an allowance of bread and water, conveyed to Halifax where he has been in prison until a few weeks since, when he was released by an order from Berkley, his crime being employed as a pilot to a torpedo boat. In consequence of his being a non-combattant our Commissary of prisoners confined at Providence by way of retalliation the sailing master of the Ramillies. This Penny is a desperado, he was 15 years an impressed seaman on board the British fleet, from which he made his escape and lived three years among the Hottentots or Bushmen where he made his escape. His adventure during these years beats Robinson Crusoe all to nothing. On his return here he swore to me that his life would be devoted to blowing up a British ship. He went on to New York and after a week or two made his appearance here again in company with a Yankee desperado. It appears that they and 7 or 8 others had conducted a torpedo boat to within 7 or 8 miles of this place, where they anchored on account of the wind. While they were here the wind rose to a tempest during which one of the men attempted to swim on shore, his comrades seeing him in danger of drowning cut the cable to give him relief, but the man drowned and the boat drove on shore among the rocks and knocked off her keel, this was in the evening, the next morning a number of the garrison started in boats to assist in getting her off, and about 9 o'clock I observed the two frigates (which lay before the harbor) make sail and steer for the place where the torpedo was. I then remarked that some rascal had given them information, which since proves to be correct; wind and tide prevented the frigates from arriving at the place until the afternoon. As soon as they hove in sight the Captain of the Torpedo after removing the apparatus into the woods, put a barrel of powder into the boat and some straw and set fire to it, but the straw being wet it did not explode under half an hour and not until after the British had landed, who however never went near it. As soon as the ship got within gunshot of the shore they opened a most tremendous fire upon the poor boat, and good old deacon Mulford's house who together with his family were 3 or 4 miles off at church. Under this fire they landed about 100 sailors and marines who soon drove about a dozen Malitia who had been firing at them into the woods and then went to the deacon's house which stood near the beach and was badly battered with their cannon balls, and after robbing it of 2 or 300 dollars in clothing, breaking the clock and looking glasses, destroying the furniture, doors and windows, proceeded to make war upon his sheep, poultry and pigs, of the former they carried off about 30 and many of the latter. They then went on board and returned to their anchorage. Thus ended the Torpedo war.

I would give you a description of this torpedo if I could intelligibly and reasonably within bounds. It is upon an entire new construction, cost $1,500 and was projected by an ingenious artist in New York at the expense of a few private gentlemen, and is I think better calculated to effect its object than any hitherto attempted. It is a bomb proof thing and calculated to go boldly up to a 74 in the daytime and blow her up. The boat will contain about 10 men, a small part of which is above water and of the thickness of

4 or 5 feet of timber and iron bars, she is kept upright by a cast iron keel, weight 1,500, is propelled by a spiral oar at the rate they say of 4 miles an hour. The contrivance of keeping off boarders and exploding their powder under the bottom of the ship is very ingenious and quite original. Poor Penny is quite inconsolable for the death of his poor torpedo, but they have promised him another.

He was so sure of blowing up the Superb and said he should then be ready to die. The Commander of the Superb however received an anonimous letter from New-York about a week before the boat arrived in these waters informing of the time she would start and her place of destination, and the next day this 90 gun ship went to sea and did not return under 10 or 12 days.

This country is full of traitors and no police. On the 4th of July a well dressed young Irishman came here in a small skiff from Saybrook, after we had eat our dinner and drank wine and toasts, the Commandant at the Garrison summoned him to examination, which I undertook. He was in Navy uniform, said he was a purser upon the Baltimore station, his name Rob. Ormby, that he had resided in Washington and Georgetown 10 or 12 years and this he made appear by his Commission from the President and a variety of other documents, from Jones, Jingy and a letter from Stephen Ormsby of the House of Representatives who is his bondsman. "How came you here? and for what purpose?" His furlow dated at Baltimore with permission to travel for his health, but this furlow was given in April and but for two weeks. "I obtained another 2 weeks more but have mislaid it." "What was your business at New London and Saybrook?" "Seabathing." For what purpose bid you come here and run the risque of capture?" "They told me at Saybrook that the best bathing was on this side of the Sound." "How long do you propose to remain here and where next?" His answer was, he should stay here two weeks and then go on to Washington through the Island by the way of New-York, that he must be at Washington by the middle of the month," but this will leave you less than no time to travel 350 miles." We examined his trunks and found them crowded with very rich clothing, all new and Navy uniforms. One coat I presume could not have cost with trimmings, less than $150, abundance of fine linen and silk stockings and $300 in specie.

The next morning he altered his mind and wished to return to New London but we told him he must pursue his first purpose and go by the stage to New York, consigned to the Marshall, where our stage driver delivered him. Before he left the place he exchanged his specie for paper. He is probably a deserter from U. S. service and his tailor, to both of whom he is in debt and going to the fleet for no very good purpose.—But I have not done with the torpedo. *Inter nos* for it is to be kept a profound secret. Poor Penny after mourning over the loss of his boat two or three weeks, received a summons from Connecticut and has obeyed it.

It appears that some Yankee projector has constructed a boat to sail under water and leisurely fasten the torpedo to the bottom of the ship and explode it. It carries two men and he has chosen Penny for one.

Doctor, I almost covet your retreat among the glens of Adams County, secure in place and plenty, while I am doomed to this sand bank in continual alarm; not a week passes but the guard boat or some of the sentinal see, or think they see an enemies barge and fire, this alarms the Garrison and the drum beats to arms, and the whole town, men, women and children are in motion.

This place consisting of about 200 houses has been built up since the Revolution by honest industry in catching whale and codfish. The people are not very rich except a few, mostly mechanics and laborers with large families. The Orders in Council put an end to all our prosperity and war is fast making them poor and wretched. It is distressing to see the changes that a few years have produced among us, perhaps near 20 of my neighbors who were formerly Captains, Mates, sailors of vessels, carpenters, sailmakers, boatbuilders, and in good circumstances are now reduced to the necessity of doing Garrison duty to get rations to feed, and a little money with which to cloath their families. We formerly had 20 or 25 coasting vessels employed in the southern trade, and in carrying wood, &c. to market. 3 or 4 of them only remain, some of them have been taken and sent to Halifax, others burnt and others so often taken and ransomed that the owners are unable to keep them in repair, and sail them, and they are either sunk at the wharf, or laid up to rot in creeks and inlets, our young men have generally gone into the Army or Flotilla service at New York, or emigrated in search of business ; nothing to be seen but houses stripped of their furniture and, as we expect to be burnt, sent out of the reach of the conflagration. Women who have seen better days are oblige to wash and billet soldiers to share with them their rations ; no happy countenances among us, but children from want of reflection and soldiers made happy by whisky ; but for our clam beds and fish many would go supperless to bed. But what is all this compared to the greatest part of Europe, devastated, brutallized and laid waste with fire and sword by a few titled scoundrels and human butchers and incendiaries. There is sure a state beyond this where such monsters will receive their punishment.

Pardon me for this long scroll and with a kind rememberance to Mrs. Crawford believe me your friend.

E. S.

P. S My health is bad, but a little better than last summer. Mrs. S. not so well generally. My children in good health and spirits.

CAPTURE OF WHSHINGTON, WAR OF 1812.

ADDRESSED TO HENRY P. DERING, SAG-HARBOR, N. Y.

WASHINGTON, Sept. 23d, 1814.

MY DEAR FRIEND :

I arrived here last Monday morning half sick from rainy weather and the vexations of delay from stage owners, Innkeepers, &c., expences of travelling are nearly double to those of last year. Our stage load was mostly members of

Congress, and on arriving at the battte ground of Bladens-burgh we surveyed it to the Capitol; it is uneven ground, vallies and high hills, thick wooded, within pistol shot of the turnpike and here and there a small cleared field; never was ground better formed for annoying an enemy, 1,000 men placed on each side of the road in the woods, would have killed every Englishman, Ross commanded, before they could have marched half way to the town. Our army consisted of about 7,000 men, Regulars, Marines and Mili-tia, 6,000 of whom never saw the enemy or fired a gun. About 1,000 of Barney, Sailors and Baltimore folks des-troyed 7 or 8 hundred of them in the first 3 or 4 miles of their march when the fatal word *Retreat* was given, and the whole army scampered off as fast as legs could carry them through George Town and over the mountains to Montgom-ery Court house, a distance of 14 or 15 miles. Had the noble General Winder gave the word Fire instead of Re-treat, it is believed by everybody a British soldier would not have found his way into the city. No one here at-taches any blame to the soldiers, they were unwilling to obey their officers but when their commander-in-chief or-dered their retreat and their officers were seen stripping off their appaulets or wraping themselves in their great coats for fear that the British sharp shooters should know them. Of these sharp shooters it appears that there was about 1,200 who were in advance of the main body, and kept up a fire upon the Malitia, but with little execution, as our whole loss does not exceed 30. The main body about 3,000 marched along the turnpike in solid columu, loaded with 3 or 4 day's provision and 80 rounds of cartridges, and shoes with wooden soles an inch thick, pricked on by their offi-cers until many of them fell dead with heat and fatigue. 14 were found in one corn field dead without any wounds. When they were shot or died on the road, they shovelled some sand over them. I counted 30 or 40 graves of this kind, many of which the hogs were rooting out, and drag-ing their red coats about the streets. We met 30 or 40 Marines with shovels going to bury them more decently.

After they had destroyed the Public buildings in the

city, four naval officers and about 100 men marched to Greenleefs point, to destroy the Arsenal, Powder Mazazine, Cannon, Barracks, and &c.

Here it appears our people had taken from the Magazine one hundred or more barrels of gunpowder and for safe keeping put it into a dry well and covered it over with rubbish. After they had set fire to every thing combustable one of the soldiers threw his match among the rubbish which took fire and communicating with the powder it exploded carrying off a column of earth 30 feet diameter, destroying 70 or 80 soldiers. I have viewed the ruins of the Public and private buildings, they are destroyed beyond any possibility of repair, especially those constructed of stone. The next morning after they were burnt, and while the stones were still hot a violent storm of rain and wind came on, and cracked and split the stones in all directions. The pillars which supported the dome of the house of representatives, and which at their base were as large as a barrel, are reduced to the size of a foot diameter, and in many places less. The amount of property destroyed public and private is immense, particularly, books, charts and public documents. The Navy Yard was devastated by our own people with a stupidity altogether unaccountable. They employed 2 or 300 men to blow up the bridge over the eastern branch which secured the British a safe entrance to the city by Bladensburgh, without any fear of our army gaining their rear; which they might have done in half an hour by passing over this bridge.

In fact the stpidity of our commanders during this whole scene can in no otherways be accounted for, but by supposing that their fears opperated so powerfully as to suspend every faculty of reflection and reason; every measure they took contributed to facilitate the progress of the enemy, they even assisted him in his work of devastation. Ross promised to respect private property and most of the citizens remained in their houses. About 200 troops only came into the city. Cockburn was the most active man in the business of conflagration, he was mounted upon a little gray mare followed by a colt, and in cantering about the streets whenever his colt was in danger of being lost he would ride back after him.

The town is full of precious anecdotes and the indignation of the people is so great against Armstrong and Winder that I doubt whether either of them could appear here in safety. The walls of the Capitol and President's house are covered with the most gross and libellous pasquinades. Three quarters of the people still believe that Armstrong sold the city to Cockburn and that everything was planned to facilitate his success; to keep up this ridiculous conceit the most ridiculous tales and falsehoods are invented and propigated, but no pen can describe the follies and blunders every day developes.

This is Friday and I expected a letter from you or some of my family, but none has come.

Remember me to your family and look out for conflagrations as Cockburn has again announced to our Government that he shall burn all within his reach.

Yours truly,
EBENEZER SAGE.

SELECTIONS FROM LETTERS.

WASHINGTON, Feb. 27, 1811.

"The Age of Wonders is not passed. Mr. Madison a few days since named Joel Barlow as Minister to the Court of France, and this day the Senate by a great majority confirmed the nomination. The wonder is that Timothy Pickering voted for him, he did more—he made a speech, in which among other good things he mentioned his religion as conducing to his qualifications. Lee, our Bordeaux Consul, told me this afternoon that he visited Timothy last evening and had some conversation with him upon the subject of the nomination. That Timothy objected to him on account of his infidelity. Lee told him that was a mistake. That Barlow was a believer in the Christian System, and was of the Unitarian faith. That says Timothy is my faith and the only true faith. Of course he supported him as being a good Unitarian, and therefore qualified for Minister plenipotentiary to the Court of St. Cloud. This is I think a judicious appointment. Barlow's long residence in Europe and being a man of letters made him acquainted with all the principle characters, particularly in France, his solid character for talents and integrity will give him a greater weight in the diplomatic circle, than any other man among us, besides he is an honest man and an American."

WASHINGTON, Feb. 24th, 1810.

"Next comes the Dutchess of Baltimore* and the Dauphin or young Napolian. She lives here in great splendor, uquipage and dress. The young Emperior has his Tutor to attend him. On Sunday she was at the Capitol, and yesterday they appeared in the Galleries. What a ridiculous set of idoliters we are. An angel from heaven would not have been more gazed at than the repudiated wife and bantling of a little yellow Corsican, because this yellow frenchman was born of the same woman who brought into existence an illustrious human Butcher."

WASHINGTON, 1810.

"We had in the house to-day a most rascally specimen of original sin and total depravity. Fulton a few days since in a letter to the Speaker requested that he might be permitted to give an explanitory lecture and some experiments of a Torpedo defence. A Committee was appointed and the letter referred to them. They reported that the house next Friday should adjourn and that he might lecture and exhibit on Saturday in the hall. It created a three hours debate and is not yet settled. Livermore, Dana, Quincy and others appeared agitated with alarms and forebodings, they made attempts at ridicule. Quincy was quite in a rage and condemned the whole system as visionary. The fact is they believe too much in it for their comfort. Fulton will risque his life on the issue that the system of defence and annoyance will one day secure the world

---

* Mrs. Jerome Boneparte, *nee* Miss Patterson, of Baltimore.

from hostile fleets. The federalists are very inconsistent in this business, for allow, (which they very much fear) that the British navy can be destroyed (which protects us from Napolion's ships) will not the same power destroy french ships as english ? But these angry zealots have long since left off reasoning.

I believe it will be permitted that Fulton should make a fair experiment upon one of the old Frigates in the Navy Yard. These anti-naval patriots of Virginia, Carolina. &c., would vote to have the experiment tried upon the whole for two reasons : that it would demonstrate the efficacy of the discovery and what to them is of nearly great importance, get rid of the Frigates."

A LETTER WRITTEN BY MRS. ABBEY LOUISA BEAUMONT, AT THE AGE OF NINETY-FOUR, TO HER COUSIN GEORGE E. LATHAM, ASKING WHAT SHE RECALLED OF SAG-HARBOR IN HER EARLY DAYS.

SPRINGFIELD. Iowa, Oct. 4, 1897.

MY DEAR COUSIN:

I was born in the beautiful village of Sag-Harbor January 22, 1803, and am now in my 94th year. Sag-Harbor, when I was young, was quite a lively place, on account of whaling ships being built and sailing out from there, some going on a three years' cruise. The great shipyard gave employment to many men.

There were only two doctors living in Sag-Harbor in my young days, Doctor Prentice and Dr. Ebenezer Sage. Dr. Sage was our family physician.

There was only one little saloon in the village, at the lower part of the Harbor, never any disturbance created by it. Every person would go to bed at night and leave their doors and windows unfastened, but in mortal terror of the British war ships in the bay, who were determined to land if possible, and burn Sag-Harbor. Many and many a time, both day and night, the alarm would be given, "the British are coming." Then the wagons would be brought to take the women and children off in the oak timber, to stay until

the cannon balls fired from the fort and wharf by our brave
soldiers sent them back. I shall never forget that six
weeks one summer, all the women and children never un-
dressed at night, but lay down with their clothes on, through
fear of the foreign foe in the bay.

The last cannon fired from the war ships in the bay at
dear old Sag-Harbor was when they were informed by two
traitors, that our soldiers were going to be disbanded on a
certain Saturday, for some reason which I cannot now remember. They were not disbanded, and now comes the
grandeur of the thing: The deceived British ships came
sneaking Sunday night a little too near, for our brave soldiers at the fort and wharf, dealt death and destruction on
board the war ships, the way the cannon balls did fly.
That was the last they fired at Sag-Harbor. If this has
never been put in history it ought to be.

ABBEY LOUISE BEAUMONT.
Abbey Latham when a girl.

In connection with the affectionate terms in which Mrs.
Beaumont refers, in her advanced age to her birth place,
it should be stated that she left Sag-Harbor when she was
eighteen years old and has never been there since, having
passed the remainder of her long life in the northern part
of the State of New-York, then in Michigan, and afterwards
in Iowa, where she now lives.

Before the attempt of the British war ships in Sag-Harbor, referred to in Mrs. Beaument's letter, Admiral Sir
Thomas M. Hardy, who had commanded Nelson's flag ship,
the Victory, at the battle of Trafalgar, was in command of
a fleet blockading New London, during which he dispatched
a boat expedition across the Sound to burn Sag-Harbor.
A sentinel on guard on Long Wharf gave the alarm of the
approach of the boats. At that time there was a high eminence close to the water, where John Homan's house now

is (1897) then known as Turkey Hill, which in the prosperous times afterwards of the whale fishery, was taken down and carried away by the whaling ships as ballast on the outward voyage. During the war of 1812 a fort for the defence of the place was erected on Turkey Hill. This fort had a nineteen pounder, and when the alarm of the approach of the hostile boats was given, a blacksmith, named Slate, hurried to the hill, quickly loaded the cannon with spikes for the want of cannon balls, and when the boats came fairly within range, he fired with such accurate aim as to strike one of the approaching boats, and it is said, killed two of the men in her. Whether this single shot did as was questioned, but whether it did or not it put an end to any further attempt on the part of the boats, and they returned to the fleet off New London.

As another means of baffling the boats, a sloop loaded with pine wood, and lying directly in line of the landing place, was set on fire, and as the boats retired from the attack, Captain David Hand, failing to get some one to join him, went alone to the burning vessel and succeeded in putting out the fire.

Sag=Harbor Portrayed in Verse.

—o—

READ AT THE OPENING OF THE SAG-HARBOR PARK, JULY 4, 1879.

—o—

There begins at the south
Of the Hudson's mouth
A long narrow tract of dry land,
That stretches before
The Connecticut shore,
What is known on the map as Long Island.

As it wends away
Toward New London bay,
In a course to the Orient trending,
It has two long prongs
Like a broken tongs,
From its eastern end extending.

The broken joint
Is Orient Point,
With Gardiner's Isle to the right on't,
Whilst the other stick
Stretches out to Montauk,
A long narrow strip with a light on't.

In the middle way
Lies Gardiner's Bay,
Protected by Gardiner's Island,
West of which, hilter-skelter,
Lies the Island of Shelter,
A jumble of bays, creeks and highland.

From the opposite shore
Cedar Point stretches o'er,
With some knarled trees forming an arbor,
And on it a light
As a guide in the night
To the innermost bay of Sag-Harbor.

Here snug and well stowed.
Like a seaman's abode,
Lies a village of three thousand people,
By the side of a ridge,
With a badly kept bridge—
And a church with a very high steeple.

This chosen retreat
Was the home and the seat
Of the bold and adventurous sailor,
And for years had supplied
To the world far and wide
The model American sailor.

Here boldly to sail
In pursuit of the whale
Was honored in every station,
And his capture and spoil
Represented in oil,
Was the thought of the whole population.

For no maiden would look
On a young man who took
To a land life of torpor and stupor,
When the scene was here laid
Of the "Sea Lions" raid,
Of our national novelist, Cooper.

Its long wharf, which then
Was well crowded with men,
Was a place of great business commotion,
Through many a ship.
Lying there to equip,
For its venturesome voyage o'er the ocean.

In these prosperous years
It had ship yards and piers,
And coopers and riggers and calkers,
Ship chandlers, sail makers,
And ship biscuit bakers,
And the whalemen then known as Montaukers.

But these scenes are all past,
And the place is at last
Like a field lying idle and fallow,
For we've found other ways
To get light in these days,
Than from oil, spermaceti or tallow.

And the whales have run out,
Or if still they will spout,
To be captured by harpoon or trigger,
The capture won't pay,
The petroleum to-day
Has brought oil to a very low figure.

As a means of bread winning
They have tried cotton spinning,
And all that the labor embraces,
But that will not stay,
And our hope is to-day,
A factory making watch cases.

Which we hope will remain
As a true source of gain,
Which nought in the future will sever;
For we cannot efface
How we love the old place—
So Sag-Harbor, Sag-Harbor forever!

[From the Sag-Harbor Corrector, July 19th, 1879.]

The following, found sticking in one of the broken rails of the bridge to North Haven, has been sent to us for publication, by the finder:

THE HUMBLE PETITION OF THE SAG-HARBOR BRIDGE TO HANNIBAL FRENCH, ESQ., COMMISSIONER OF HIGHWAYS.

———o———

Oh, Hannibal French! Oh, Hannibal French!
  Give ear to this earnest petition,
For nobody wishes you here to retrench,
  While I'm in this wretched condition.
The half of my planks are all worn and decayed,
And great gaping fissures between them are made,
Whilst holes in some places are opened to view,
Where the leg of a horse can go easily through,
So that horses approaching, with fear and with dread,
Go picking their way, sadly shaking their head,
And saying, as far as they are able to say,
This is Hannibal's way! This is Hannibal's way.

And should no impression be made in the least,
By the constant complaining of man and of beast,
Then I call to my aid your historical name,
And bid you remember great Hannibal's fame,
Who crossed o'er the Alps, though the snows were impeding,
His bold Carthagenians successfully leading,
As did also Napoleon, with whom you may claim,
Some connection at least, from the French in your name.
And if they with great armies could cross mountain ridges,
You surely could mend up the humblest of bridges.

Whilst Nickerson's yard is abounding in hoards
Of the very best planks and the strongest of boards,
My only defense to the dash of the spray,
Is some rotten old boards that are crumbling away.
My foot-planks, in part, are but worn out old slips,
The relics, I am told, of some broken up ships,
That rattle and jolt when a wagon goes by,
With their ends all devoutly turned up to the sky,
As saying, in view of their services past,
Oh, Hannibal French! how long will this last?

Old friend, I should think the delight of your days,
Would be the employment of mending your ways,
Or if to such mending you do not incline,
I wish you would take to the mending of mine,
Or a horse will be damaged, in going across,
When the township, you know, has to pay for the loss,
And that's not the pleasantest thing to display,
When all is made known upon Town Meeting day,
And every one quotes in the old-fashioned rhyme—
What is saved by a stitch that is taken in time.

And Hannibal French, beware of the day,
When the Storm-King shall come in his fearful array,
And exposed to his terrible blast,
My shattered old fabric shall give up at last.
    When 'mid loud peals of thunder,
    My beams gape asunder,
    And lightning is flashing,
    And timbers are crashing,
And I finally fall from a terrible wrench,
    With one piercing cry,
    Going up to the sky,
Of Hannibal French! Oh, Hannibal French!

The reference in the foregoing verses to a "badly kept bridge" was the bridge to North Haven, which in the year 1879 was so neglected that it became dilapidated and dangerous, and led to the publication of the above *jeu d' espert*, the effect of which was that the Commissioner of Roads repaired it so that it lasted until the present fine structure was erected, at a cost of $23,000, $18,000 of which was contributed by Sag-Harbor's public spirited citizen, Joseph Fahys, Fsq.

www.ingramcontent.com/pod-product-compliance
Lightning Source LLC
Chambersburg PA
CBHW020037030726
47499CB00007B/2461